A Rabbit's Eyes

by Kenjiro Haitani
translated by Paul Sminkey

VERTICAL.

Published by Vertical, Inc., New York.

Originally published in Japanese as *Usagi no me* by Rironsha, Tokyo, 1974.

ISBN 1-932234-21-7

Manufactured in the United States of America

First American Edition

Vertical, Inc.
257 Park Avenue South, 8th Floor
New York, NY 10010
www.vertical-inc.com

CONTENTS

A Rabbit's Eyes

Prologue

Tetsuzo's case begins with a tale about flies.

Ms. Fumi Kotani, Tetsuzo's homeroom teacher, who had gotten married only ten days earlier, was a recent graduate, and so was completely blown away by Tetsuzo's behavior. Rushing into the teachers' room, she threw up violently and burst into tears.

The astonished Assistant Principal raced to the classroom to investigate and found Tetsuzo glaring at something on the floor. The other children were screaming and yelling. Glancing down at the boy's feet, he initially thought he saw some kind of colorful fruit, but when he took a second look, he unconsciously let out a yell: it was a frog crushed in two, the twitching innards scattered upon the floor like a red flower. For a moment, he stood paralyzed, but when he noticed a little girl crying and petrified with fear, he realized he had to dispose of the mess immediately. When he pushed Tetsuzo aside to get to work, however, he discovered another crushed bullfrog under the boy's right foot.

Ms. Kotani mulled over the incident for a long time. You couldn't kill something so cruelly if you didn't have a lot of anger. Wait a minute. Tetsuzo lived at the garbage disposal plant right behind the school, didn't he? With all that garbage, there had to be plenty of flies. Perhaps he had had a fight with one of his classmates about collecting flies to feed to the frogs.

Ms. Kotani had good reason for her supposition: a recurrent problem at the school was that the disposal plant children were often called "garbage collectors" and other similar names. Just the same, she couldn't know for sure. Even if he had been teased, why did he have to kill those frogs? She questioned many students about where they had collected food for the frogs, and two admitted that they had gone into the compound. One of them had found four or five flies on a pile of garbage, and the other had found thirteen flies "inside a bottle," next to the home of a family who worked at the plant. At the time, Ms. Kotani thought the part about the bottle was strange, but she dismissed her doubts for the moment and moved on with her questions.

Certainly, it was strange to say that you caught thirteen flies "inside a bottle." Were the flies inside the bottle already? Of course, it would be possible to collect them one by one, from various bottles lying around, but even so, it sounded strange. If only she had investigated further, she certainly would have discovered the truth.

The two students said that Tetsuzo hadn't shown them into the compound. They said that he didn't have any friends and that he had stopped helping with the frogs at the start of using "live food." But they also admitted that he had never fought with anyone. In the end, Ms. Kotani didn't discover a thing.

The next incident occurred about two months later, during a class on observing ants. Ms. Kotani was explaining that the best way to get the ants to nest was to wrap a black cloth around the observation bottle. She indifferently picked up the bottle of a student in the front row to demonstrate when, no more than a few minutes into her explanation, she suddenly found Tetsuzo leaping at her like a hunting dog.

Ms. Kotani shrieked instinctively, but having done so, she was no longer a teacher: she was just a young woman named Fumi Kotani. In a frenzy, she shook Tetsuzo off as if he were some kind of vermin. The students were aghast at Tetsuzo's sudden attack on their teacher, but when they saw him snatch the bottle from her hand, they understood.

The bottle's owner was Bunji, and he became the next target. By the time he started to scream, his face was already covered with blood. With the skin hanging down in shreds, the scratches made his face look like a rag splotched with red paint. As Tetsuzo's onslaught continued, Bunji tried to shield his face with his hand, but Tetsuzo sunk his teeth into the boy's hand. Bunji let out a violent scream, and as Ms. Kotani tried desperately to pull Tetsuzo away, she caught a glimpse of the white bone of Bunji's hand and fainted.

Afterwards, in the teachers' room, the Assistant Principal slapped Tetsuzo to the floor. The other teachers didn't criticize him for his violence, for they had seen Bunji carried away to the hospital with blood dripping from his face and hands. Tetsuzo refused to explain himself—no matter how many times he was slapped. He didn't even cry. Witnessing such stubbornness, even the female teachers, who at first felt sorry for him, began to think that the violence towards him was unavoidable.

Ms. Kotani was recovering in the nurse's office, so the

Assistant Principal took Tetsuzo home. He scolded the boy in front of his grandfather, whose full name was Baku Usui but whom everyone called "Mr. Baku" on account of his unusual first name. Still, Tetsuzo refused to speak.

Ms. Kotani took the next day off. And the day after that. Three days after the incident, she finally went back to work. Although she had the reputation of being a pretty teacher, she didn't look at all attractive upon her return.

Shortly after noon that day, Mr. Baku came to the school to speak with her. What he had to say disconcerted her, and she spent a long time reflecting on his words. She could hardly wait for the students to be dismissed before rushing to the hospital to see Bunji. She woke him up and asked him whether the flies were already in the jar when he found it at the disposal plant two months earlier.

"Yeh, they were," he said quietly.

"Why did you take them? They were Tetsuzo's," she said, with an edge of annoyance in her voice. "It was a Chinese jam jar and had a strange shape, so he recognized it right away. You used it for your ant observation jar, didn't you?"

"I'm sorry," said Bunji with shame, and his teacher's stern look softened.

Bunji admitted that he took the jar because it was full of flies, but said that he hadn't known it was Tetsuzo's.

"I want you to apologize to him, understand?" said Ms. Kotani, and it was as if she had decided something for herself as well.

The next day, she called Tetsuzo to the teachers' room.

"I really have to apologize," she began. "You were collecting flies, weren't you? You saved them in a jar. You were worried about the frogs not having any food, and when the flies you collected disappeared, you got mad. I should've tried to understand your feelings. I'm truly sorry."

Tetsuzo listened unresponsively, in silence.

Like horseflies, misunderstandings often come flying from unexpected places. The next day, Bunji's father stormed into the teachers' room and created an uproar.

"Not only was he attacked," he yelled, grabbing Ms. Kotani by the collar, "but you've told him to apologize to the kid who attacked him! What's the meaning of that!" Unaccustomed to such violence, Ms. Kotani turned pale and lost her voice.

As the Assistant Principal rushed over to intervene, Bunji's father tried to punch him, and when a young teacher prevented that, the father knocked a cup of hot tea on him. Finally, the enraged father was maneuvered into the principal's office, where the Principal tried to talk to him, but the man was raging out of control and wouldn't settle down. Somehow or other they managed to quiet him down with an explanation, by which time Ms. Kotani's makeup was running down her face, and she appeared on the verge of a breakdown. The Principal knew that she had been brought up as the sheltered only child of a small-town doctor, and he worried that she wouldn't be able to bear the shock.

That evening, the Assistant Principal escorted Ms. Kotani home as if she were a small child.

In the morning, after a sleepless night, Ms. Kotani groaned like a wounded animal that she was going to quit. The other teachers, however, easily squashed her request, and one colleague teased her, saying that if everyone who wanted to quit were allowed to do so, in ten years there wouldn't be a single teacher left.

But Ms. Kotani felt that working at this school had somehow made her heart grow cold. When she realized that even students that she had at first considered adorable might, over a slight misunderstanding, hurt her, she knew she had to be on guard. Everyday, she came to school feeling depressed.

The school was in an industrial zone. Soon after getting off at the train station, as you approached the school, you were engulfed by a haze, which all day long smothered the area in a gloomy gray. Ms. Kotani always felt slightly dizzy when she arrived. Since the school was located right next to a garbage disposal plant, it suffered much damage. The disposal plant was constructed in 1918 and had barely received any improvements since. For that reason, the smoke coming from its chimneys was intense, and the smell was horrible. When the ash was being removed, white dust would rain down on the school and the nearby homes alike. The lower-grade students would sing laughingly about the "falling snow," but the situation infuriated the older students, who had even submitted a letter of protest to the local government.

Of course, there had been frequent plans to move the disposal plant to another location, but the plans never seemed to materialize. Before elections, every political party pledged to relocate the plant, but since the plan was never once carried out, the townspeople referred to the plant as the seventh natural wonder of the town.

To give a short description of the plant, there were three furnaces for burning trash, all of which were rather simple contrivances: the openings to the furnaces were on the second floor, and the garbage collected there was simply shoved down into the furnaces below. Before incineration, the garbage was roughly divided into burnables and non-burnables. Garbage more difficult to burn would often smolder, and there was nothing to do but wait for it to burn out. And so the furnaces' efficiency would vary considerably, depending on the type of garbage. Usually, it took twenty-four hours to burn one load of garbage. The ash would drop down and accumulate in some sort of underground room, which had a door facing the street, so the ash could be easily taken away.

Ash-removal was carried out in the morning. The workers, who wore nothing but loincloths because they were soon covered with ash, appeared rather gallant to passers-by, but the work could be extremely hazardous because aerosol cans would sometimes explode and pieces of glass would sometimes cut the workers' hands and feet. Garbage that couldn't be immediately disposed of was collected in a large gymnasium-like building next to the incinerators. During the rainy season, the heat of the rotting garbage made the entire room stifling.

Standing slightly removed from this building was the housing for the plant workers: a harmonica-like tenement house holding fourteen or fifteen homes. Tetsuzo's home was on the easternmost end. Generally speaking, there were two groups of people working at the disposal plant. One group, who were city employees, did paperwork inside nice concrete buildings, or supervised those working at the plant, and when evening came, they headed off to their respective homes. The other group, who were merely temporary workers, did the manual labor at the plant. These people sorted and burned the trash, and took away the ash. They were the ones who lived in the tenement house in the middle of the compound.

Having come to the school next to this disposal plant, Ms. Kotani could understand, when she considered all of the incidents that occurred during the first four months up until summer vacation, why the children living in this area were the way they were. There had been four traffic accidents—an average of one per month—and although fatalities had been avoided, one child had been hospitalized for six months when he was hit by a car and dragged nearly thirty meters.

There was also a serious non-traffic injury: a boy had fallen from the roof of a steel mill while trying to get a pigeon that had settled there. The incident made headlines in the local newspapers, and the school's responsibility was questioned. For the school, it had been the major incident of the year. Every month, there were several cases of shoplifting from the supermarket, and one month there were as many as ten. There was one case of a student running away from home, and many cases of parents abandoning their children, so many that it was impossible for the school to investigate them all. And there was another incident: a catastrophe was once narrowly averted when a vagrant who had entered the school grounds tried to abduct a female student.

Compared to all these problems, the scene caused by Tetsuzo was quite ordinary and normally wouldn't even have been considered an "incident." The only reason it attracted so much attention was that Ms. Kotani was a brand-new teacher.

It truly was a troubled school. Even some of the teachers were strange. One day, Ms. Kotani wanted a second opinion on some student essays. She considered asking Mr. Adachi because he had written some poetry and composition books for children, but she was hesitant because he had a bad reputation. He had long hair, and the clothes he wore were far from the standard attire of a suit and tie. She thought he was a bit of a slob. On top of this, there were rumors that he gambled and that his personal life was in disarray. And yet, for some reason or other, the other teachers respected him. She vaguely remembered hearing that this was because he was popular with the parents.

In the end, she decided to show him the essays. When she entered his classroom, she found him lying across a string of small desks that he had lined up in a row. She was shocked. She had heard that he was called the "mafia teacher," and the nick-name seemed to fit.

"Mr. Adachi, do you always sleep like that?" she ventured to ask.

"Yeh, I guess," he responded, spitting the words out at her. But then, he sat down on a chair like a normal teacher and began to read. He smiled as he read the essays. "These are pretty good. There's probably other undiscovered treasure, too."

"I'm not quite sure what you mean."

"I mean your students probably got good stuff in them, even though you might be overlooking it. And I don't mean just com-positions."

His comment disconcerted her.

"Oh, and by the way, you seem to be having a lot of trouble with Tetsuzo Usui, but from my experience, he's the kind of kid who's especially full of treasure."

Ms. Kotani was surprised. It wasn't particularly strange that he had heard about the incident with Tetsuzo, but at a school of nearly two thousand students, it was impressive that he would know the name of a student in another grade. She was happy to hear him praise her student, but she didn't really understand what he meant. He had said that Tetsuzo was full of treasure, but what treasure could he have been referring to? Tetsuzo never wrote or spoke, so where could his treasure be hidden?

1. A Rat and a Yacht

Summer vacation came to the school and to the children living near the disposal plant. Without children, the school was soon covered in dust, turning musty like an old castle. At the disposal plant, on the other hand, the garbage began to ferment in the heat, and the entire compound turned as hot and humid as a greenhouse. But even in such discomfort, the children played cheerfully.

Tetsuzo received a letter from Ms. Kotani, and Mr. Baku read it for him.

Dear Tetsuzo,
How are you doing? I've been worried about you, but when I remember you feeding the tadpoles, I tell myself that you must be fine. I'm doing very well. I feel like I'm a college student again, and I've gotten quite tan vacationing in the mountains and on the ocean. I'm looking forward to seeing you for the second semester.

Sincerely,
Ms. Kotani

"She's a nice teacher, isn't she?" said Mr. Baku. Tetsuzo

hugged his dog, Lucky, and looked off indifferently.

In the small open area in front of Tetsuzo's house, Isao, Yoshikichi, Jun, Shiro, and Takeo were playing catch. Jun missed Shiro's throw, and the ball rolled into a gutter, which was really more of a large sewer flowing into the nearby canal. Jun plunged in after it and before long, reappeared clutching the ball, his face grimy with mud.

"Hey!" he yelled, throwing the ball back. "There's a big rat with silver eyes in there."

"Liar!"

Stung by the accusation, Jun yelled back, "If ya think I'm lying, come see for yourself!"

The entire group scampered down into the gutter. Shiro got out first, and Isao followed. Their eyes met, and they heaved a sigh.

"Hey, he wasn't lyin'," said Isao. "It's gotta be the king of all rats."

The game of catch came to a quick end, and the children decided to try to capture the rat alive. After a short consultation, they scattered off in various directions, and before long, they reassembled, each child armed with netting, a sieve, wire, elastic, or some other essential item. Shiro, the last to arrive, was nearly in tears, apparently having met with some resistance for stealing the cheese they undoubtedly intended to use as bait.

The children quickly rigged up a rattrap, and even Tetsuzo, whom the children called "Tetsutsun," was enlisted in the effort.

"Tetsutsun, could ya hold here?"

He pressed down his finger, and the cheese was tightly tied down with string. The trap was designed so that the metal netting would fall down with even a slight tug on the cheese. When it was finished, Jun climbed down to place it inside the gutter.

"It might not be the rat with the silver eyes that takes the bait, though," said Isao.

"That's true," muttered some of the others, worried.

"The guy with the silver eyes is king," said Jun, as he climbed out of the gutter. "So if there's anything good to eat, he's gonna be the one to get it."

They nodded in agreement, unfazed by the fact that their grimy faces looked like old maps dipped in muddy water.

The children waited for nearly an hour, their eyes wide in anticipation, until finally, unable to endure it any longer, they jumped down into the gutter together. Only Tetsuzo—the first-grader—watched from above.

"Darn it!" one of them yelled, and the brigade trooped back out again. Though they had used rather durable string, it was completely gnawed through in the middle.

"He didn't even pull; he just chewed right through it. Boy, he's smart!" said Yoshikichi, in admiration.

"Yeh, not at all like you," said Isao.

"What'd ya say?" said Yoshikichi, scrunching up his face.

For their second attempt, they constructed a hook out of the wire, and positioned the bait higher than before, so that the rat would have to hold the cheese with its front feet in order to eat. The new incarnation of their ingenuity was quickly returned to the middle of the gutter.

"What'd ya think, Tetsutsun? Will this do the trick?" Jun asked.

"Uh," Tetsuzo answered. The short groan was impossible to interpret, but that was always how he answered, so Jun and his friends didn't mind. They spoke to their uncommunicative friend just to be nice.

The children sat down in a circle in the shade. They had no desire to engage in other play while they waited, and with furtive glances, they communed in silence about the rat with silver eyes. After a while, Jun, the one reader in the group, began to tell about Ernest Thompson Seton's *Lobo the Wolf: King of Currumpaw*. As they imagined Lobo, overcoming the traps of hunters, one after another, shivers ran down their spines. The story heightened the thrill of trying to catch the rat with silver eyes, and their hearts throbbed with excitement.

"Haven't we waited long enough?" asked Shiro, in a shaky voice.

The other children nodded, but they had mixed feelings. They desperately wanted to catch their prey, but they didn't want it to be too easy: he had to be a tough and stubborn enemy. With Jun taking the lead, they jumped down into the ditch, and listened in silence as they kicked and splashed through the water.

"We did it!" Jun screamed in a high-pitched voice, and everyone was startled. They ran up to feel the trap and could feel the weight of the rat banging against it. They were ecstatic.

"He's huge!"

"It's definitely the King of Rats!"

"It's him! It's him!"

"It's the rat with silver eyes for sure!"

Their throats were soon parched as their excitement reached new heights.

"Are his eyes shinin'?" asked Isao.

The children peered through the darkness and made out two silver orbs, less than a quarter of an inch in size, flitting about in the darkness. Unable to constrain himself, Yoshikichi gave a shout of joy, and before long, the narrow tunnel was reverberating with the yells of rejoicing children.

Tumbling out of the gutter, the children respectfully lifted the great king above their heads and hurried him away in procession. Lucky leapt out of Tetsuzo's arms to give chase, and Tetsuzo took up the rear.

The children's hideout was located on the westernmost end of the compound. Though made of old wood, the result far exceeded what you would expect from children, so that even adults contemptuous of such play would allow it to remain standing. The coolest place in the compound, the children's "fort," as they called it, served as a headquarters for planning pranks and as a temporary shelter for when they were thrown out of their homes.

It was to this holy place that they brought the King of the

Rats. After lowering the cage to the ground as if it were some fragile object, they gathered around and riveted their gazes. God had revealed Himself, and the hot stares of His admirers threatened to send Him up in flames.

Some time passed.

Jun sat down first, and then Takeo. He sat across from his friend and looked him in the eye. They had identical expressions, and neither one of them had anything to say. Isao and Shiro figured it out next, so that only Yoshikichi and Tetsuzo were left.

"His eyes were silver when he was in the gutter, right?" asked Yoshikichi, finally catching on. "Why aren't they silver now?"

"You idiot!" answered Isao with annoyance. "When animals are in the dark, their eyes shine when the light hits 'em."

No one blamed Jun. Drained of their strength, they absentmindedly gazed up at the sky.

"So what do we do with 'im now?" Shiro asked, after another long silence.

"Let's kill 'im," said Yoshikichi.

"Poor thing," muttered Tetsuzo, who was still staring at the rat.

"Yeh, that's right," said Jun, smacking Yoshikichi on the back of the head. "But, of course, since he's a rat, we can't just let 'im go." He looked around to the others for suggestions.

"Let's wash 'im down the river," said Isao, and it was settled.

With the same eagerness as they had built the trap, the children set to work on constructing a small wooden box. They placed some cheese inside, so that the rat wouldn't starve, and carried the completed box to the canal. They set the box in the water, and carefully, so that he wouldn't knock into any rocks, they set him adrift.

While Tetsuzo and his friends were sending the rat down the canal, Ms. Kotani was sailing on a yacht in the ocean. She was having so much fun during the summer break that it led to arguments with her husband. She herself thought it strange to be so lost in having fun, and wondered if it might not be an unconscious attempt to forget her first painful months of teaching. Having grown up in a doctor's household, she had always been rather studious and preferred reading to playing outside. As a college student, traveling with friends had been her one and only diversion.

"Going wrong" was an expression that was often applied to students that suddenly turned delinquent, and perhaps Ms. Kotani was "going wrong" in her way because of the four stressful months of teaching. As soon as summer vacation started, she headed to the Nagara River in Gifu with some teachers from her school. After that, she immediately took a trip to the Japan Alps, where she climbed Mt. Kasaga. When August came, she hurriedly put her schoolwork in order and headed off to the American Village, a beautiful fishing village in Wakayama Prefecture with houses of white stucco walls and black tiled roofs.

But nothing she did for fun satisfied her. During her years in college, she always enjoyed her trips and never felt an urge to travel again once they were over. Now it was different. Even if she didn't have a good time, she felt a desire to head back out again. But why?

And now, with summer vacation nearly over, she was sailing on a yacht in the ocean. Something strange happened during the trip. On the way back from the Ejima Islands in Hyogo, they were sailing into Himeji's Murozu Port when she noticed a black object floating in the ocean. They pulled alongside and lifted out what turned out to be a turtle, about one foot in length. From its size and shape, they could see that it wasn't a sea turtle, and for some odd reason, it had a two-inch-long tear on the right side of its belly. The wound had healed and didn't seem to pose a threat to its life, but why was he swimming in the ocean? And where was he trying to go?

The turtle swam with his neck stretched out and his legs flailing, but in the middle of the vast ocean, his struggle seemed ridiculous. And yet, precisely for this reason, Ms. Kotani was moved by his futile determination.

2. Mr. Adachi, Mafia Teacher

A smog warning had been in effect, but the sky was transparent blue, a sign that autumn was approaching. No one complained when smog forecasts missed the mark. The weather had the children wound up, and Ms. Kotani's voice rang out from the first-grade classroom. She was teaching her students how to tap out rhythms with their castanets.

"Just relax, and if you can't do it, try to catch the beat with your body."

Her decadent summer lifestyle had made her more lenient.

"And don't copy your neighbor. That just makes you fall behind, and then it gets all messed up. If you can't do it, just move your head. Okay, let's begin. One, two, three. One, two, three . . ."

The high-pitched clicking echoed through the classroom, and the students and their teacher were in high spirits. Just then, the door opened and Mr. Adachi's head popped in.

"I wish you'd at least knock," hollered Ms. Kotani, rather annoyed.

"I wish you'd at least knock," mimicked a mischievous student, and everyone laughed. Mr. Adachi stuck out his tongue at the boy, and the laughter grew louder.

He quietly relayed his message, and Ms. Kotani's brow darkened.

"I'll see you later, then," he said.

"Okay," she answered.

On his way out, he made fun of her.

"If you can't do it," he mimicked, "try to catch the beat with your body."

Ms. Kotani turned red.

As Mr. Adachi headed out the door, several students yelled after him.

"Come again!"

"See you later!"

He really was popular.

"Well, the disturbance is over," said Ms. Kotani, somewhat chagrined, "so let's get back to work."

The castanets rang out again, and as usual, Tetsuzo sat at his desk doing nothing.

"Tetsuzo, how about trying it with me?" she asked. Then she wrapped her arms around him from behind and took his hands in hers. "One, two. One, two. One, two, three. One, two . . ."

Tetsuzo reluctantly tapped out the beat with his teacher.

"I'd like you to try it by yourself next time, understand?"

She went back to the front of the class and began conducting. Not surprisingly, Tetsuzo sat motionless. She sighed.

While she had been holding him, she noticed that his hair smelled. She had nearly said something, but she stopped herself. That was not something you could say to a boy without parents.

Now she had two chores to do after school before returning home today.

At four o'clock, she left school with Mr. Adachi and headed to the Harukawas. Kimi Harukawa was in Mr. Adachi's second-grade class, and Satoshi, her younger brother, was in Ms. Kotani's first-grade class. The children's mother had abandoned them for the second time. According to Mr. Adachi, she was not likely to return this time.

He had spoken with their father about the situation and had thought that everything would be okay, but today, the school received a complaint: in flagrant violation of school policy, Kimi was charging children in the neighborhood ten or twenty yen to help them with their studies. Mr. Adachi didn't believe it at first, but when he thought it over, he realized it might be true.

He explained that many families in the school district were poor, but not all of them, and that although some just barely managed to make ends meet, others were flashy with their wealth. He pointed out that in such an environment, ugly things were bound to happen, and that children might imitate what they saw.

As they approached Kimi's neighborhood, the number of noodle shops, bars, cheap grilled-meat restaurants, and *okonomiyaki* joints increased. Mr. Adachi turned into an alley and ducked into a *taikoyaki* shop, apparently to buy some treats for his visit. While the *taikoyaki* muffins were cooking, he chatted away with the shopkeeper. He was usually rather quiet at school, but he sure seemed to enjoy talking now. What a strange fellow!

In the entranceway to Kimi Harukawa's apartment, there was

a wooden sign that read "Violet Contemporary Housing Complex—Vacancies Available." The hallways were dark, which made it difficult to see.

Mr. Adachi stood in front of the sign and shook his head. "Pretty classy name for a place like this, huh?"

Ms. Kotani giggled.

Kimi Harukawa turned out to be a delightful little girl. As soon as her teacher walked through the door, she jumped on him and climbed up on his shoulders. As Ms. Kotani gazed in amazement, Kimi sat on her perch and began drumming on Mr. Adachi's head.

"Baldy, baldy, completely bald . . . " she sang.

"Hey, what're you callin' me that for? You call a handsome teacher names, and he's not gonna give you any *taikoyaki*."

That finally got her to climb down, but then she wrapped her arms around his neck, and whispered in his ear, "Is Ms. Kotani your girlfriend?"

"That's right," he said jokingly, "but don't tell anybody at school."

"Okay, but it'll cost ya three *taikoyaki*'s," said Kimi, indefatigably cheerful.

"What's your little brother up to?" asked Mr. Adachi.

When Kimi said he was outside playing and offered to go get him, Mr. Adachi looked to Ms. Kotani for the answer, and she whispered so that Kimi wouldn't hear, "It'd probably be better without him."

As Kimi ate a *taikoyaki*, Mr. Adachi casually chatted with her.

"So you've been helpin' some kids with their studies, huh?"

"Yeh," said Kimi, still looking down. "I taught 'em how to make some pictures, too."

She was trying to anticipate his next question, which made her look precocious.

"What kind of pictures?" he asked, trying to put her at ease.

"Those decalcomania ones ya taught us about."

Decalcomania are mirror-image pictures made by folding two or three different colored paints inside a piece of construction paper.

"Yeh, I'm sure you could've managed that."

Mr. Adachi picked up a *taikoyaki* and started eating. He asked Ms. Kotani to have one, too, but she politely refused.

"Who'd you teach?"

"Ma-chan, Shige-chan, and Kotoe-chan."

"How much did ya get?"

Mr. Adachi asked in a lighthearted way, but Kimi started to fidget.

"Twenty yen."

"From each of them?"

"Yeh."

"I see," said Mr. Adachi, looking off into the distance for a minute. "So how's your dad?"

"He came home yesterday, but he was away for three days."

"Why didn't you say anything at school?" he asked, somewhat

harshly.

Kimi didn't answer.

"So how much did he leave for you?"

"Five hundred yen."

"Was that the same day you got twenty yen from Kotae-chan?"

Kimi nodded, and it was painful to witness.

"Oh, Kimi," said Ms. Kotani, calling her by name.

She stopped eating her *taikoyaki.*

"Kimi," said Mr. Adachi.

"Huh?"

"No more accepting money, okay?" He spoke with lighthearted sympathy.

"Yeh," said Kimi, with a nod.

Ms. Kotani was filled with emotion. When she considered that Kimi was still at the age for cuddling up with her mother, the tears began to well up in her eyes.

On their way back to school, Mr. Adachi looked annoyed, and by the time they reached the busy part of town, his expression had grown even sterner.

"How about a drink?" he asked suddenly, darting into a bar without asking whether Ms. Kotani had plans. She was planning to go to Tetsuzo's house, and she knew she'd regret it if a parent saw her going into a bar with a male teacher, but she didn't want to leave him in the lurch, and she had many things she wanted to ask. She made up her mind to go in.

Mr. Adachi's glass was half empty by the time she entered, and when she sat down next to him, he acted like he didn't notice her. Lost in thought, he restlessly poured the liquor into his body.

"Is Kimi always so cheerful and gentle?" she asked.

"No," he spit out. He had turned ill-tempered again, and Ms. Kotani became afraid to talk to him. Around children, he was lighthearted and cheerful, but this was a completely different person.

"Oh, uh, sorry," he said, suddenly coming to himself.

Thinking how strange he was, Ms. Kotani fought back the desire to laugh.

"When you're with Kimi, you really make yourself understood—even though you don't say much. Like today, you didn't really say much, but she knew she had done something wrong, and apologized."

"I don't know about that," he snapped at her. "Was it really so wrong?"

He tossed down his drink and continued.

"It's not something people like us can comprehend, but Kimi must've been ecstatic when she got that sixty yen. If her dad doesn't come home tonight, and they can't eat, that sixty yen will come in pretty darn handy—even if she had to do something naughty to get it."

Perhaps because he was getting drunk, more of the local Kansai dialect[1] was slipping into his speech.

"If she could talk like an adult, she'd have said something like

'Hey, I taught 'em the best I could for only sixty yen, so what's wrong with that?' Would ya've had a comeback for that?"

Mr. Adachi was getting drunk, but he spoke calmly.

"Kimi didn't apologize 'cause she thought she did something wrong. It was 'cause a teacher she liked, for some unknown reason, told her to stop. One of the two people in the world that still care about her told her to knock it off. So of course she agreed. She probably didn't feel like she had much choice."

Ms. Kotani's eyes were riveted on him.

3. Tetsuzo's Secret

Ms. Kotani said goodbye to Mr. Adachi, and with a heavy heart, rushed off to see Tetsuzo. She felt insignificant compared to the heroic student and teacher she had just left and depressed that her visit to her own student probably wouldn't accomplish anything.

When she arrived at Tetsuzo's house, she thought that he was playing by himself, but she was mistaken: he was picking off the fleas swarming on Lucky.

"Tetsuzo!" she called.

He glanced over at her and then turned back to his dog.

An image of Kimi climbing up on Mr. Adachi's shoulders flashed into her mind, and the contrast saddened her. When would Tetsuzo ever start talking to her?

She went to the door and caught Mr. Baku unawares. He had just returned from work at the disposal plant and was starting to clean himself up—even his eyelashes and nose hairs were dyed white from the ash. When he saw her in the doorway, he hurriedly washed his face and threw on a shirt.

"Tetsuzo," he called loudly, "it's Ms. Kotani!"

"Mr. Baku," she began, trying to sound upbeat and casual, "would you mind if I washed Tetsuzo's hair?"

"Ooh," said Mr. Baku, emitting a strange sound. "We're not really into bathing. I'm sorry about that."

He acted as if he had done something wrong, and Ms. Kotani

didn't know what to think.

"I'm going to wash your hair for you," she said to Tetsuzo when he came in from outside, "so come with me to take a bath."

Tetsuzo stood staring at the ground, but she ignored his reaction and went to prepare the bath. She walked out the back door and found a concrete patio that was just the right size, but when she went to carry out the washtub, Mr. Baku became extremely flustered. First he grabbed the tub away from her and carried it out himself, and then he tossed a tent-like cloth over some object that was on the corner of the patio.

"What was that?" she asked.

"Oh, nothing, nothing," he mumbled, as if the question disturbed him.

Ms. Kotani figured that it was a plant or something.

When the bath was ready, Tetsuzo quietly took off his clothes and reluctantly climbed into the tub. His head hung down in silence. "Tetsuzo, do you go to the bathhouse by yourself?" asked Ms. Kotani.

He didn't answer.

"Or do you go with a friend?"

Again, he was silent.

"Who are some of your friends?"

After her third failure, Ms. Kotani gave up asking questions.

"I don't like baths, either," she said. "My hair's long, so it takes a long time to wash. It's a real pain. That's why I hate baths—just like you."

Tetsuzo pulled his legs to his chest and dropped his head.

"Wow, Tetsuzo," said Mr. Baku, coming alongside the tub, "you're lucky. You really owe her for this one."

He doesn't owe me anything, Ms. Kotani thought, but I wish he'd at least speak.

Before long, Tetsuzo's skin had turned pink and shiny.

"Look at that," said Ms. Kotani, slapping him on the back. "You're really handsome now."

He didn't even crack a smile.

Ms. Kotani tripped over something as she went to put away the tub, and even though Tetsuzo still didn't have his shoes on, he quickly ran over and stuffed the object under the heavy cloth. It looked like a bottle.

After that, the atmosphere amongst the three of them turned sour, and it wasn't until three days later, as a result of an incident with two other disposal plant children, that she discovered Tetsuzo's secret.

Isao and Yoshikichi had to collect fruit flies for a science experiment at school. Since they lived at the disposal plant, where there were many flies, many of their classmates begged them to collect their share, too.

Fruit flies are not easy to catch: only about three millimeters in size, they are crushed if you grab them with your hand, and they escape through the holes if you use a net. The only way to catch them is to use bait.

Isao and Yoshikichi tried soybean paste first because that's what they learned at school, but some chemical substance in the paste—either the preservative or the coloring—seemed to scare the flies away. After that, they tried various kinds of fruit, and when that didn't work, they turned to dried fish and mackerel heads. They lived next to a lot of garbage, so they knew what flies liked. The fish attracted many flies, but there wasn't a single fruit fly in the bunch.

"It's useless," said Yoshikichi, at his wits' end. "Why don't we just ask Tetsutsun?"

As sixth-graders, they felt funny about asking a first-grader for help.

"I guess we don't got any choice," said Isao.

Yoshikichi ran off to get him, and when they returned, Tetsuzo picked up the jar they were using and tossed out the fish parts.

"I guess we aren't usin' the right bait, huh?" asked a disheartened Isao.

"Uh," answered Tetsuzo, in his usual incomprehensible way. Then he scurried off, and Isao and Yoshikichi, who were twice his size, toddled along behind him.

When he reached the garbage dump, Tetsuzo started searching for rotten pieces of fruit. He sniffed each piece he found, and if it passed his test, he handed it to one of the older boys. Extremely rotten pieces didn't seem to pass. Yoshikichi took a sniff of one he had been handed and noticed that it had a sour-sweet smell with a slight scent of alcohol. The fruit had just started to ferment—not that Tetsuzo could have known such a difficult word.

Using the new bait that Tetsuzo collected for them, the boys had a jarful of fruit flies in no time.

"Wow!" said Isao, thoroughly impressed.

"That's Tetsutsun, for ya!" said Yoshikichi.

The compliments didn't faze Tetsuzo in the least.

At school, Yoshikichi blabbed the story to some of his friends, and by the time Isao tried to tell him to shut up, it was too late.

"How could a first-grader know so much about flies?" asked Isao's teacher.

"Now what'm I supposed to do?" grumbled Isao.

He reluctantly explained to his teacher that Tetsuzo raised flies as pets and that he knew so much about flies that the plant children called him the Fly Professor. He also had to tell him that Mr. Baku knew all about it, but that he was keeping it a secret so that Tetsuzo wouldn't get in trouble at school or be bullied by his classmates.

Isao glared at his friend when they got together at the end of the school day.

"You idiot," he said. "Don't expect me to bail ya out."

Yoshikichi looked dejected.

Ms. Kotani was informed at once, and when she heard the news, she immediately recalled the incident with the frogs. Bunji had said that he found some flies in a bottle, but he had probably inadvertently stolen the flies that Tetsuzo was raising—bottle and all.

She called Yoshikichi and Isao to the teachers' room to ask them why Tetsuzo was raising flies.

"What'd ya mean, 'why?'" asked Isao, confused. "Tetsuzo loves his flies—just like somebody that's got a pet parakeet or a goldfish."

"Except that birds and goldfish are expensive," put in Yoshikichi, "and flies are free."

The teachers sitting nearby burst out laughing.

"But flies are covered with germs," said Ms. Kotani, with a look of disgust. "Why would he want to have such an unsanitary pet?"

"I got no idea," answered Isao, completely flustered. "Why don't ya go ask him yourself?"

As a general rule, the disposal plant children used the same casual language with their teachers as they used with their friends. Isao was still annoyed at Yoshikichi, and while they spoke to Ms. Kotani, he occasionally poked his friend in the ribs. With each poke, Yoshikichi looked crestfallen.

Ms. Kotani finally understood why Tetsuzo had crushed the frogs: the flies were his pets. Bunji didn't know that when he fed them to the frogs, but when Tetsuzo saw his pets being eaten, he got angry and took revenge against the frogs. That also explained why Tetsuzo stopped taking care of the frogs after they started being fed live food.

Yet when she thought the matter through, she sensed that this only created another problem: raising animals or plants was one thing, but raising flies was quite another. Tetsuzo was only a child, so he probably didn't have personal hygiene in mind when he started raising them.

The whole thing gave her a headache. When she recalled how energetically Tetsuzo had crushed those frogs, she knew it would be difficult to get him to give up his flies. Just the same, she was determined to talk the situation over with Mr. Baku. But then she remembered something else: when she had gone to their home to give Tetsuzo a bath, Mr. Baku and Tetsuzo had conspired to hide something. And that bottle was probably filled with some of his flies. But why on earth would Mr. Baku let his grandson raise flies?

Ms. Kotani left school at three o'clock to meet Mr. Baku at the disposal plant. It was so hot that no matter how many times she wiped her face, the sweat kept dripping down. When she entered the disposal plant compound, the fermenting garbage made it feel even hotter. She couldn't help thinking how utterly absurd it was to be raising flies in such a place.

Before her visit, Ms. Kotani had checked out a book on flies, and she became especially upset when she read sentences such as this: "Numerous viruses that are spread by flies have been cited from long ago: paratyphoid, salmonella, cholera, amoebic dysentery, various parasitic diseases, tuberculosis, and more than twenty other diseases, including dysentery and typhoid fever. Current research also strongly suggests that certain species of blowflies are carriers of polio." She would have to explain all this in language that Tetsuzo could understand.

When she arrived at the disposal plant, Isao and Yoshikichi spotted her immediately and came running over. Jun, Shiro, and some others followed.

"Don't get mad at Tetsutsun, Ms. Kotani," Isao pleaded frantically. "His dog and his flies are his only friends. Please don't get mad!"

"I didn't come to yell at him," she replied. "I just wanted to ask him and his grandfather why he's raising flies."

"Well, that's okay, I guess," said Isao, sounding like an adult. "But really, Ms. Kotani, his only true friends are his flies—not that a pretty lady like you'd have anything to do with dirty things like flies."

"Don't try to butter me up," said Ms. Kotani, giving him a playful shove. He giggled and took her arm. Yoshikichi and Jun giggled, too, and pressed up close as they walked along.

Ms. Kotani couldn't believe how friendly they were. Some teachers said horrible things about the children living at the plant, but Ms. Kotani couldn't see it.

"Do other teachers come here often?" she asked.

"You gotta be kidding!" yelled Shiro, in a shrill voice. "Most of 'em just make fools of us. They say we stink and that we're stupid. They don't even treat us like human beings!"

Shiro's harsh words sent a chill down her spine. What could drive such pleasant children to talk like this?

"Even though they're the ones that bring their stinkin'

garbage here!" "That's right!" piped in the others.

"The only good teachers at Himematsu Elementary School are Adachi, Orihashi, and Ota."

She was pleased to hear Mr. Adachi's name.

"Mr. Adachi's okay?"

"Yeh, he's our friend. Isn't he, you guys?"

"That's right, he's our friend," said the others.

"What about Ms. Kotani?" she asked.

"She's okay," said Isao, a bit embarrassed.

"What's okay about her?"

"Well, you're really fond of Tetsutsun, aren't ya?"

Ms. Kotani was taken aback, and then felt self-conscious.

"Tetsutsun's weird, so you're probably havin' a tough time," said Isao, sounding mature again.

"Yeh, that's right," said Ms. Kotani, beginning to adopt their informal way of speaking. "I'm having a tough time with him."

"You smell good," said Jun, bashfully.

Ms. Kotani felt more relaxed with the children backing her up, and she decided to see Tetsuzo before talking with his grandfather. She slipped around to the back of the house.

Tetsuzo was sitting against the wall, with his arm bent and raised to eye level. He was staring at some objects on his arm, and Ms. Kotani strained to see what they were. When she realized that innumerable flies were dancing up and down his arm, she nearly screamed. How could such a thing be possible? They were swarming on his arm like bees around a hive. They didn't try to fly away, but clung to him like spoilt children. She assumed that he had plucked off their wings, but when she moved closer to confirm her suspicion, she could see that he hadn't.

"Tetsutsun!" called Yoshikichi.

Tetsuzo glanced over towards them, and when he noticed that Ms. Kotani was with them, he jumped up and hid his arm behind his back.

"It's too late, Tetsutsun. She already knows," said Isao, apologetically.

Ms. Kotani grasped Isao by the shoulder and timidly edged towards Tetsuzo.

The flies were a shiny yellowish-green, nearly half an inch in size, and looked like toys made out of glittering metal. Ms. Kotani didn't know it, but they were green bottle flies.

"They're pretty, aren't they?" said Jun, innocently.

As far as Ms. Kotani was concerned, nothing could've been further from the truth. She had goose bumps running up and down her arms, and her hands were starting to shake.

"Tetsuzo!" she yelled, as if delirious. "Get rid of those! Right now! Geez!"

Tetsuzo began putting the flies back into the bottle one by one.

After she finally settled down, Ms. Kotani asked the question that had been on her mind.

"Why don't they fly away?" she asked.

"Hold on," said Isao, running off.

He soon returned with a fly that he had caught.

"This is a regular fly," he began, "so if I let 'im go, he'll fly away. But look here: under these large wings, there's another set of smaller wings. Can you see 'em?"

She saw what he was talking about and nodded.

"And right below those wings, there's this little thread-like thing. Ya gotta look real close, or you won't see it."

"I see it," she said.

He borrowed the tweezers from Tetsuzo and pulled off the thread-like objects under the wings.

"Now watch this," he said, dropping the fly to the ground.

The fly still had wings, but when it tried to fly, it immediately toppled over and floundered on the ground.

"Tetsutsun would say he's dancing."

Forgetting how creepy it was, Ms. Kotani was impressed.

"Tetsutsun showed us how to do it," said Isao, with a guilty look.

Altogether, Tetsuzo had about twenty bottles of flies, which when lined up on the empty tangerine box looked like specimen bottles at a hospital. Ms. Kotani wondered how many different species he had collected. There were motionless bluish-black ones, clinging to the wall of their bottle, and large striped ones, bustling about like greedy little things. The shiny indigo-colored ones, shooting about sharply, seemed to be the liveliest of the bunch.

The only species that Ms. Kotani had ever heard of was the

housefly.

"I wonder how many species he has," she said. "And which ones are the houseflies?"

"There aren't any," answered Isao. "Tetsutsun says they eat people's crap and are dirty, so he doesn't raise 'em."

In addition to the adult flies, Tetsuzo was also raising pupas and maggots. The sight of them made Ms. Kotani feel sick to her stomach again, and when she thought that physical contact with Tetsuzo might not be possible for her anymore, she felt utterly wretched. She regretted having come today at all.

Mr. Baku was extremely embarrassed about having caused her so much trouble and after deciding something for himself began to tell her the entire story.

"I really didn't mean to hide anything from you, but you've been so nice to him and all, and if you had found out about the flies, well . . . And then, with you being a young female teacher, I just couldn't bring myself to tell you. Not only that, but I've heard that the kids living here get bullied a lot, and if Tetsuzo got bullied over such a thing, it would be a real shame, so I went and kept it a secret.

"When I first found out about it, I got pretty angry myself. I don't usually spank him, but I spanked him that time. And I smashed all his bottles, too. But no matter how angry you get, and no matter what you do to him, Tetsuzo's gonna raise his flies. After a while, I stopped getting mad, and I stopped hitting him. He doesn't have a mother or father, and he doesn't have anyone to really love him. So I just didn't think it was worth getting mad at him anymore. I told him to go ahead and raise his flies if he liked them that much. But I also told him that people hate flies and that he shouldn't let anybody see what he was doing.

"Ms. Kotani, Tetsuzo's not raising flies because he's bad. If I took him to the mountains, he'd start collecting insects. If I took him to a river, he'd want some fish. But I can't take him anywhere, and the only place he knows is this trash dump, and there's nothing here but some bugs and flies. It's only natural that he's raising them.

"I should've told you everything when he got violent with that Bunji kid. It was wrong of me to hide everything about the flies and just tell you about his bottle getting stolen. But one of Tetsuzo's favorite flies was in that bottle. He called him 'Kinjishi,' the golden lion, and it was a magnificent fly. Most flies, even if they're big, are no more than half an inch or so, but Kinjishi was almost an inch long. He was shiny and gold and haughty like a king. When he was stolen, Tetsuzo was really upset and didn't eat for a day. I felt bad when he hurt that kid Bunji, but considering how he loved that fly, I figured he'd do something at least that bad.

"I'm sorry he's been so much trouble for you, but I'm not telling you all this so you'll feel sorry for him. Tetsuzo's a human being, and I just wish he had a human friend. He's a human being."

Ms. Kotani was speechless and stared at the ground.

4. A Bad Day

Just as bad weather usually continues for two or three days, misfortunes often follow one after another.

On Wednesday, Ms. Kotani attended the weekly teachers' meeting. After all the scheduled discussion items were finished, and everyone was thanking God it was over, the Assistant Principal jumped to his feet.

"Just one more thing," he said. "I had a request from Ms. Murano, and she'd like to discuss something with you. I'd appreciate it if you could give us a little more of your time. Well, then, Ms. Murano."

Ms. Yasuko Murano, the head teacher for the third-grade students, turned pale as she began to speak.

"There is a child in my class named Koji Senuma."

Many teachers rolled their eyes when they heard the name: Koji was one of the disposal plant children.

"The other day, I consulted with the other third-grade teachers about whether I should allow Koji to help serve lunch. I should point out that Koji is incapable of cleanliness: he doesn't wash his hands before meals, he won't use the antiseptic lotion, and his hands and feet are always dirty because he hates to bathe. I've tried everything, but he hasn't improved. I've also contacted his parents and asked for their help, but they don't return my calls and don't seem to be concerned. Recently, the other children have been complaining, and refusing to eat their lunches when

Koji's serving them. I've been very strict about hygiene, so I can't very well ignore their reasonable excuse for not eating. If by any chance there was a case of food poisoning, I'd be responsible. I've spoken to Koji about this many times, and I told him that if he didn't change, he wouldn't be allowed to serve lunch. But when I brought this up with the other third-grade teachers, Mr. Orihashi told me that my policies were discriminatory. Now, I've been teaching for twenty-five years, and I feel that I've done my best, but this is the first time I've ever been accused of discrimination, and I just can't accept Mr. Orihashi's one-sided accusation. That's why I'd like to get your opinion and find out what should be done in this situation."

"Mr. Orihashi, do you have anything you'd like to say?"

"I don't know what to say," said Mr. Orihashi, scratching his head in confusion. "I'm only in my second year now, so unlike Ms. Murano, I don't really know a lot of stuff and can't really say this is good or this is bad, and, uh . . ."

Apparently speaking wasn't Mr. Orihashi's forte, and with the sweat dripping from the end of his nose, he was obviously put out.

"I guess I just wanted to say that nobody in the class, not even Ms. Murano, was looking at things from Koji's point of view. I can't really express myself well, but I don't think Koji's dirty because he wants to be, and if you look at it from his point of view, I think you'd see things differently. I'm not a very good speaker, so I can't really say anything profound."

Mr. Orihashi sat down, and the other teachers smiled. He was sweating so profusely that they couldn't help but feel sorry for him.

Ms. Murano jumped up immediately.

"And what's that supposed to mean? I took this measure precisely because I *am* looking at things from Koji's point of view. If I didn't do anything, he'd end up being even more of an outcast. But since he's the cause of the problem, if you ignore that cause and look at it from his point of view, you won't solve anything. Mr. Orihashi likes to pretend that he's so concerned about the children, but it really just turns out to be another case of sparing the rod and spoiling the child. True education sometimes requires a degree of strictness."

After this, several teachers stood up and spoke. Most of them were sympathetic to Mr. Orihashi but sided with Ms. Murano on the issue at hand. The consensus was that while it was important not to hurt the child's feelings, it would be a mistake to overlook filthiness.

One teacher said, "I have my students vote to decide who will serve the lunches, and I encourage them to vote for someone who's considerate of others and whose appearance is always clean. Since that becomes the goal, everyone wants to be chosen, and they compete amongst themselves in a positive way. I think that's very educational."

During a break in the comments, the Assistant Principal turned to Ms. Kotani.

"How do you deal with Tetsuzo Usui?" he asked.

Ms. Kotani was startled. She had been dreading that the discussion might turn to Tetsuzo.

"I let him serve lunches just like everyone else," she answered in a whisper.

"He raises flies, doesn't he?"

Ms. Kotani felt as if she were sitting on needles.

"You let that Usui kid serve lunches!" exclaimed Ms. Murano, in disbelief. That Tetsuzo was raising flies had become common knowledge amongst the faculty.

Ms. Murano then maliciously asked the school nurse what she thought about letting such a child serve school lunches. Of course, the nurse said that that was going too far, and that they should put an end to it immediately. Ms. Kotani felt quite small.

"What the hell are you talking about!" someone exclaimed.

It was Mr. Adachi.

"If you'd like to say something," said the Assistant Principal, in a huff, "please raise your hand first."

"Me, please!" mocked Mr. Adachi, in an even louder voice.

Grudgingly, the Assistant Principal told him to go ahead.

"What Mr. Orihashi said is right," Mr. Adachi began, "and what everyone else said is wrong. Every student should be given a turn serving lunch. While it's fairly obvious, Koji and Tetsuzo are both students, and if they spread germs because they're dirty, then everyone in the class, including the teacher, should be happy to get infected."

The other teachers burst out laughing.

"I'd appreciate it if you spoke a bit more seriously," said the Assistant Principal, making a sour face.

"I *am* speaking seriously, and what I want to say is this: I'd like each of you to ask yourself whether you aren't just using health issues as an excuse for trampling on the feelings of your students."

Ms. Kotani raised her hand.

She stood up and remained silent for a moment, searching for the right words.

"I'm embarrassed that I didn't think the matter through when I had Tetsuzo serve lunch. I admit that he's dirty. I was shirking my responsibilities to let such a student serve lunch without a passing thought. And before anything else, I'd like to reflect on my behavior."

"No need to do that," heckled Mr. Adachi.

"Quite some time ago, there was an incident where Tetsuzo crushed some frogs. At the time, I was so terrified that I couldn't imagine what he could be thinking or feeling to do such a cruel thing. But the other day, I found out the reason."

She explained in detail how she discovered Tetsuzo's secret and gave a full account of what Mr. Baku had said.

"Tetsuzo still hasn't opened his heart to me, but there's nothing I can do about that. He's a good kid. If I had been more in touch with his feelings when that first incident occurred, the past four or five months wouldn't have been such a waste. I really regret it. From my experience, I can very much understand what Mr. Adachi and Mr. Orihashi were saying about valuing students' feelings. Tetsuzo has been using the disinfectant, thank goodness, so I hope you'll allow him to continue serving lunch. As for his raising flies, I'll do my best to persuade him to stop."

Ms. Kotani had never spoken at a teachers' meeting before, so the other teachers listened in complete silence. When she finished, her body was shaking, much to her embarrassment.

The first bad thing that happened on this bad day occurred after the meeting. The Assistant Principal called Ms. Kotani to a nearby classroom, and when she arrived, he stood glaring at her.

"I'm not too pleased with what you said at the meeting, Ms. Kotani," he said with disgust. "You make me sound like an ogre, but I went to a lot of trouble for you when that happened. The way you describe it, I frivolously hit Tetsuzo Usui for no reason at all. Is that what you think?"

Ms. Kotani didn't know what to say and stood rigidly in silence. The whole experience left her feeling crushed.

The second bad thing occurred on the way home from school when she went to have a talk with Tetsuzo. Even in her dreams, she didn't think she'd be able to get him to give up his flies right away, but she thought she might be able to get him to loosen up a bit. Her plan was to be patient, for she couldn't forget what Mr. Baku had told her.

"Tetsuzo's a human being," he had said, "and I just wish he had a human friend."

When she entered the disposal plant compound, Isao and his friends came running up as before. It hadn't taken much effort to get on friendly terms with them.

"Isao, what kind of kid is Koji?" she asked.

"He's right here," said Isao, pointing to a little boy standing next to him.

"You're Koji Senuma?" she asked.

"Yeh," said Koji with a big nod, and he smiled at her with his big brown eyes.

Ms. Kotani couldn't believe it. At the teachers' meeting, she had imagined some extremely disgusting brat. From the way they talked about him, you would have expected him to be a gloomy, defiant kid that was always giving nasty looks. But the real Koji was nothing like that. Certainly, he was barefooted and dirty, but this amount of dirt was typical for a child living in the city. Even with her pale complexion, Ms. Kotani herself would get just as dirty if she played barefooted.

"You have pretty eyes, Koji," she said, and he smiled.

"Pretty popular with the ladies, huh?" Jun teased, and Koji beamed with delight.

"Damn!" Ms. Kotani muttered to herself. "That old maid fooled me!" The bad habits of Mr. Adachi and the disposal plant children were starting to rub off on her.

"Ahem!" rebuked Isao, throwing out his chest and mimicking the Principal. "That's not the proper language for a teacher."

Ms. Kotani gave an embarrassed laugh.

"Tokuji's coming home tomorrow, Ms. Kotani," said Shiro, who was Tokuji's best friend.

"Is that right? So he's leaving the hospital tomorrow? That's great."

Tokuji was the boy who had fallen from the roof of the steel mill while trying to get a pigeon.

"I wonder how he'll look when he gets out."

The children were very worried about him.

"So did ya come to see Tetsutsun?" asked Isao.

"Yes," she answered, and it occurred to her that instead of talking to Tetsuzo alone, it might be better to try to include him in a casual chat with the group. "Could you go get him for me?"

Jun ran off to get him, and while she was waiting, Ms. Kotani spoke with Koji.

"Koji, do you like taking baths?"

"No."

"But if you don't get clean, you won't get a girl to marry you."

Koji giggled in embarrassment.

"Do you wash your hands at lunch time?"

"No, but . . ."

"But what?"

"Everybody says I got cooties."

"Who does?"

"Everybody."

"Doesn't your teacher yell at them?"

"She's on their side. She says I'm bad. She says I'm bad 'cause

I'm not clean."

Ms. Kotani sighed.

"I see. And that's why you don't wash your hands?"

"Yeh."

"Well, how about if I tell your class how you feel?"

"No, that's okay."

"Why not?"

"'Cause I hate Murano."

It occurred to her that Tetsuzo probably said the same thing about her. "I hate Kotani," she could practically hear him saying, and the thought depressed her.

Just then, Jun returned with Tetsuzo, who was the same old soulless doll as ever. When Tetsuzo appeared before his teacher with his head hanging down, even Jun was appalled.

"You really are unfriendly," he said.

"Jun, could you take me to your hideout?"

"My hideout?"

"You wrote about it in writing class."

"Oh, our fort."

The children were thrilled to take Ms. Kotani to their bungalow.

"Hey, it's really cool here," she said, when they arrived.

"It's the coolest place in the compound."

"It sure is."

"Adachi comes here all the time. He takes naps here when he's cuttin' teachers' meetings."

Ms. Kotani burst out laughing. He truly was a recalcitrant teacher.

"You always call your teachers 'Adachi' or 'Murano,'" she said, raising an issue that had been bothering her. "So do you always call me 'Kotani'?"

Isao scratched his head.

"Now that you mention it," said Shiro, "you're the only one we don't call that way."

"That's right," chimed in the others, with puzzled looks.

"Why is that?" she asked. "It doesn't seem fair."

"It's a special bonus 'cause you're pretty."

"You're just saying that because you want me to get you something, right?"

"Adachi always gets us *taikoyaki*," blurted out Yoshikichi.

"You idiot," said Isao, quickly poking him in the ribs. "I can't believe you."

Ms. Kotani laughed to herself. It never took long for these two to move into their comedy routine.

"It's okay," she said. "But *taikoyaki* is hot, so let's have Popsicles instead. I'll treat."

The children shouted for joy.

Ms. Kotani really felt relaxed talking with them. She knew she wasn't Mr. Adachi, but she felt sure that if she spent time chatting with them like this, Tetsuzo would open up to her eventually.

They sucked on their Popsicles happily, including Ms. Kotani, who polished one off like a child. The children took their time.

"The teachers were talking about you today, Tetsuzo," said Ms. Kotani. "And they all know that you're raising flies."

Isao glanced over at Tetsuzo.

"Flies are covered with germs, you know. I checked it out myself and found out that they carry dysentery, typhoid, and other really scary diseases. Now if you caught one of those diseases from your flies, and then served lunch to everybody at school, what do you think would happen? That's right: everybody in class would get sick. That's why the teachers are worried. Now, there are lots of other nice bugs you could raise, Tetsuzo. Some that you've probably never heard of. So how about we look for a new pet together? One that doesn't hurt people."

Tetsuzo stopped eating his Popsicle.

"Even now, right here in this town, there's a campaign to get rid of flies and mosquitoes. They're spreading insecticide that will kill as many as possible."

Ms. Kotani didn't catch the glint in Tetsuzo's eyes.

"Because if they don't kill the flies . . ."

Tetsuzo stood up and walked right up to her. Then he grabbed her face and thrust her away with all his might. Ms. Kotani screamed and tumbled backwards.

"Tetsutsun!"

Isao jumped up with a red face, and Tetsuzo ran away.

It happened so fast that Ms. Kotani didn't know what hit her. In a daze, she watched Tetsuzo fade into the distance, and when he vanished, the dam inside her broke and flooded her with sadness and emotion. Her chest grew hotter and hotter until it hurt, and then everything went blank.

She sobbed loudly like a small child, oblivious of the children crouching at her feet. Isao and Jun stared at her with tears in their eyes.

The third bad thing occurred when she returned home.

Completely drained, Ms. Kotani plopped down on the floor in the living room without even turning on the lights. She didn't even realize her husband was home until he spoke to her.

"What's for dinner?" he asked.

"I haven't decided yet," she answered languidly.

When he turned on the lights and saw her face, he was taken aback, but when he heard her explanation, he dismissed the problem and told her to just forget it.

"I'm upset because I can't forget it!" she yelled hysterically.

"You're acting silly," he scolded her. "You really need to get your priorities straight. How are you supposed to take care of somebody else's kid when you can't even take care of your own home?"

Tears poured from her eyes.

"If you were living on your own," he continued, "you could do whatever you wanted. I have unpleasant things happen at work, too. But what do you think would happen if I brought all those problems home with me? You really need to start thinking about why we're living together."

She knew that they were growing apart. She wanted to say that his idea of "unpleasant" was completely different from her own, but she didn't say another word.

That evening, Ms. Kotani gulped down quite a bit of whiskey. She felt totally and completely alone. As she was drinking, a fly stopped on the rim of the whiskey bottle, but instead of shooing it away, she stared at it. For what seemed like ages, she gazed at the lone fly.

5. A Pigeon and the Ocean

Tokuji returned home from the hospital. If Tetsuzo was the Fly Professor, then Tokuji was pigeon crazy, and the first thing he started talking about was his birds.

"How's Kintaro?" he asked, referring to his favorite bird.

"I've had a hard time with 'im," answered Shiro, who had been taking care of the pigeons while Tokuji was away. "He's been bullyin' the others, so guys like Gonta can't get anything to eat or drink."

Of the approximately fifteen pigeons, Gonta was the oldest.

Everyone went with Tokuji to see the pigeons, which he kept in a coop at the side of his house.

The coop had been destined for destruction after Tokuji fell from the steelworks roof and seriously injured himself, but when he heard about this plan in the hospital, he flew into a rage.

"Go ahead and try to destroy it!" he screamed, picking up the fruit knife on the table and waving it in the air. "But if you do, I'm gonna die!" Worn down by the impassioned plea, Tokuji's parents relented and enlisted Shiro to help.

Tokuji beamed with delight when he saw his pigeons again.

"There's Taro! And there's Chonko! Hey, Donbei! Look over here! Look who's back!"

Before long, one of the pigeons started cooing, and that set off a chain reaction, so that the entire coop was soon cooing away.

"They remember me!" squealed Tokuji, his face aglow.

"They're happy to see me again!"

"Yeh, I didn't know pigeons were so smart," said Isao, sounding impressed.

"So which one's Kintaro?" someone asked.

Shiro pointed to a pigeon that did indeed seem without foe. Unlike the others, who glanced around nervously, Kintaro stared straight ahead. Shiro put in some food and water, and the pigeons immediately flocked to the food and started eating.

"Now watch this," he whispered.

Kintaro glanced back and forth a couple of times, flew up into the air, and came swooping down to the trough like a bomb. As soon as he landed, he started pecking the pigeon next to him. The pigeon jumped to the side and tried to continue eating, but then Kintaro attacked in earnest: he climbed on the other bird's back and began pecking away at his neck. When the bird tried to run away, Kintaro chased after him and violently stabbed at him with his beak.

"Boy, he really is nasty," said Jun, hating to see a weaker animal be bullied.

"Is that Gonta?"

"Yeh, he's the guy gettin' beat up."

Shiro reached into the coop with a stick and knocked Kintaro away.

"Gonta's gonna get weaker," said Tokuji, sounding worried.

Driven towards the nesting box, Gonta was puffed up like a ball, and his down had lost its luster. Keeping an eye on Kintaro, he waited for an opening and rushed back to the trough. He had barely eaten a couple mouthfuls of food before Kintaro was attacking him again.

"He's so vicious!" said Isao, frowning.

"Tokuji, you should evict 'im," said Jun.

"Yeh, maybe we should," said Shiro.

"Evict him!"

"Put him out!"

With all of his friends in favor, Tokuji felt backed into a corner, and in the end, he relented.

Shiro knocked Kintaro through the trapdoor with his stick, and the evicted pigeon soared high into the air.

"The nitwit's happy about it!" said Shiro with annoyance.

One of the pigeons inside the coop started cooing.

"That's gotta be his girlfriend," said Shiro, and the children felt a pang of remorse.

Kintaro alighted on top of the highest rooftop in the compound.

"He's glancin' around like he's nervous."

"He's in shock, I bet."

Kintaro didn't budge from his perch, and the children, who were expecting him to fly away, exchanged glances.

"It's like he's been made to stand out in the hall," said Takeo.

"I guess that's why ya can relate to 'im," Isao teased, and Takeo began to sulk.

"Oh, let's forget about 'im."

The children tried hard to do just that. At Tokuji's house, they played *fumawashi*, a game where you race *shogi* pieces around the outside track of the board. They made an unspoken agreement to avoid all mention of the banished bird, but their eyes kept drifting to the window.

"I'm gonna go take a pee," said Shiro, and the others looked at him with suspicion. "Just a pee," he shot back.

When he returned, they started another game of *fumawashi*, but none of them got into the game.

"I'm gonna go take a pee, too."

This time it was Isao.

"Me, too."

As Isao and Jun stood next to each other urinating, they glanced up at the rooftop out of the corners of their eyes.

"You're not peein' all that much," said Isao, and Jun turned red.

They headed back inside together, each keeping a close watch on the other.

When yet another boy tried the same trick, Tokuji couldn't stand it.

"No fair, you guys!"

That was the tip off, and the children made a dash for the door, each fighting to be first.

Kintaro was still perched on the top of the roof with the wind blowing against him. In his seclusion, he seemed like a different pigeon. Shiro turned away and kicked a stone as hard as he could.

The next day, the children woke up early, and with sleepy eyes, glanced up to the rooftop. Kintaro was still there. Relieved, they ate breakfast and headed to school.

At school that day, none of them could concentrate on their studies. Shiro was made to stand out in the hall twice, and Isao made an incoherent answer to one of his teacher's questions and was laughed at by his classmates. Jun did worse than usual on his math test, and Takeo got in big trouble for knocking over a milk carton during lunch.

As soon as classes were over, they made a dash for home, praying that their fears not be realized. When they entered the compound, they quickly glanced up at the rooftop.

Kintaro was gone! The children were dejected, for they knew that it was too late to take back their words of condemnation.

At about three o'clock, all the children assembled. It was unfair to Tokuji to leave things as they were. They asked him about likely places to find pigeons and made a special point of remembering Kintaro's characteristics. The plan was to split up into several search parties and to report any sightings to Tokuji. Since he still hadn't fully recovered from his injury, he was left behind to serve as headquarters.

At about four o'clock, the children trickled in one by one, their faces blackened with sweat and dirt. Reports were unnecessary, for their exhausted faces told the story of failure. Breathing heavily, they plopped down on the ground, their eyes still burning with resolve.

"Oh, there's one more place pigeons go," said Tokuji.

The children jumped up immediately.

"It's so close, I almost forgot about it, but ya know that flour mill out by the ocean at the end of the canal? Well, there's a wheat silo there, and pigeons go there all the time. Kintaro probably got hungry, right? Well, maybe that's where he went."

The children were convinced and felt that they would find Kintaro in a minute if only they went to the mill. They broke into a run.

To reach the canal, you had to go out the front gate of the disposal plant and then circle around, but the impatient children didn't hesitate to take the shortcut through the sewer. They entered the same tunnel where they had captured the King of the Rats, and when they came out at the other end, they scaled the fence of the car factory and jumped into the vacant lot of the quarantine station. The rest of the way was easy, so they finally stopped running.

"I wonder if Kintaro's mad at us?"

"Yeh, he flew away sulkin'."

"Do ya think he'll commit suicide?"

"You idiot! Pigeons don't commit suicide!"

"Well, dogs do. I saw it with my own two eyes. He was dragged in by the dogcatchers, and when they threw 'im in the cage, he bit off his own tongue."

"Wow!"

Chattering boisterously, the children reached the ocean,

which stretched out before them like a vast wasteland. Just then, the evening sun was sending out streams of vermilion that rippled across the ocean like ripe ears of rice swaying in the wind. The never-ending murmur of the waves seemed to be whispering to them, and for a short while, they stood enchanted by the scene. The ocean was usually a dirty, dark gray, so they felt as if God were playing a trick on them.

The flourmill's silo, reaching up towards the heavens, stood out conspicuously. They scaled another fence and edged towards the storehouse.

"We gotta be careful that guy don't catch us," Isao warned.

A huge flock of pigeons covered the back of the storehouse roof.

"Wow!" blurted out Yoshikichi in surprise.

The pigeons began cooing restlessly with the approach of the unexpected intruders.

"How many do ya think there is?"

"Oh, I don't know, about a hundred."

"Naw, there's gotta be at least two hundred."

The children spoke in whispers, but they knew it would be close to impossible to find Kintaro. Even so, they searched assiduously.

"Hey!"

A loud voice rang out, and the children jumped up. The frightened pigeons rose up into the air with a tumultuous rush of flapping wings, and together with the children, they frantically fled the scene. The pigeons, however, had no fear of being reported to the school, nor did they dread being endlessly lectured in the teachers' room.

Yoshikichi tripped as they were making their getaway, but when Isao yelled and kicked him in the behind, he managed to get up and keep running, half in tears. They struggled to climb the fence, and once they were over, they threw a parting shot at the security guard who was chasing them.

"Hey, fatso, if ya don't like it, why don't ya come and get us?"

All of them had escaped, but their attempt to find Kintaro was over, and they were disappointed. On top of that, Yoshikichi's knee was bleeding.

"Don't be such a sissy!" Isao scolded, but he felt like crying himself.

When they reached the landfill, they sat down facing the ocean. A chilly wind had started to blow.

"Hey, look at that!"

The children looked to where Takeo was pointing and saw a flock of about two hundred pigeons banking sharply. They were flying off to the west and cast a beautiful silhouette against the sky, which was dyed deep red from the setting sun.

Jun let out a big sigh.

"Those guys can go wherever they want," said Shiro, enviously.

"I wanna go somewhere, too," said Isao, in a subdued voice which was unusual for him.

"I wonder what's on the other side?" one of them asked.

"Across there?"

"No. Way, way over there, I mean."

"It's the Mediterranean Sea."

"No, it's not. It's the Indian Ocean."

"You're both wrong. It's the Atlantic Ocean."

"Shut up, you guys," said Jun, "anywhere'd be good." Then he murmured, in a soft voice, that he wanted to go somewhere that was open and wide.

"Jun, do ya like the ocean?" asked Isao.

Jun nodded and recalled the story of Moby Dick. Jun's ideal of manhood was Ahab, the whaling ship captain who swore revenge against the ferocious white whale that had eaten one of his legs.

"I like guys that're real men," he said. "And the sea turns ya into a real man."

The children reflected on Jun's words as they gazed across the ocean and dreamed of faraway places. The sun tumbled into the sea and tinted their faces red.

They were late in returning, so Tokuji came out to meet them. It was hard for them to look him in the eye.

"I'm really sorry, Tokuji," Shiro apologized. "But we bombed."

"Hey, it's all right," said Tokuji, trying hard to sound cheerful in an attempt to lift their spirits. "I don't mind."

The children traipsed into the compound as if they were

returning from a funeral. They gave one last futile glance towards the rooftop, but as they expected, there was no sign of Kintaro. The fool had run away for good, and he didn't even know how they felt. He was such an ingrate.

"Hey, Tokuji!" Shiro yelled in a piercing voice. "Look at that!"

A lone black shadow was perched on the clothesline at the side of Tokuji's house.

"It's Kintaro!"

Everyone yelled and ran to see, but since they didn't want to scare him away, they let Tokuji climb up quietly by himself. He lifted the trap door, and Kintaro nonchalantly dropped down into the coop.

Tokuji yelled down to Shiro and the others, who were waiting.

"Kintaro's come home!"

6. The Fly's Dance

Piled up on Ms. Kotani's desk were several books that she had been poring over for quite some time, occasionally taking notes. She looked so intent that the teacher next to her became curious and asked what she was reading. She whispered that it was a secret and turned her eyes back to her desk.

The books were about insects and included an illustrated guide and a reference book on breeding. She had skimmed through all of them looking for information on flies and was shocked at how little she found. Even though flies are intimately connected to our lives, extremely little has been written about them. The books in the school library were useless, and of the five books she borrowed from the public library, only two were technical books on flies. Since one dealt solely with classifications, she was left with only one book that looked promising, and it wasn't even written by an entomologist: a Department of Agriculture official who did research on seafood chanced upon the subject out of a need to prevent food contamination resulting from fly infestations. Strictly speaking, you couldn't even say it was about flies.

It was surprising that human beings were so ignorant about flies, and Ms. Kotani suspected that no one in the world had detailed information. She herself had always believed that flies eat bacteria, but this was a huge mistake. Many teachers tell their students that eating bacteria is why flies are dirty, but this was just a matter of passing on mistaken information. What they should tell their students is this: flies enjoy foods covered with bacteria, so rotten food or anything unsanitary should be thoroughly disposed of before flies come in contact with it. She began to feel that flies had been given a bum rap.

Her desire to read up on flies had sprung from her argument with her husband. After being violently pushed by Tetsuzo, and coldly rejected by her spouse, she was feeling completely alone, and as she was drinking out of despair, a lone fly had stopped on the rim of her bottle as if to comfort her. It might have been that she was drunk or perhaps because she was crying and needed a kind word, but she felt very close to that fly.

As she read, she came across a couple of interesting facts, which were so exciting that she was just dying to tell someone. She glanced around the teachers' room and noticed that Mr. Adachi was still at his desk. She turned a bit red at having thought of him so quickly.

"Do you have a minute?" she asked him.

"Sure," he answered, taking a break from his work.

"It's rather unusual for you to work so late, isn't it?"

"So it would seem."

Although teachers were expected to stay until five, Mr. Adachi never did, which was one reason why he had a bad reputation with so many of his colleagues.

"How did you get that cut on your face?" he asked, with a mischievous grin. It was a subject Ms. Kotani had been hoping to avoid.

"Well, it wasn't my husband," she answered, trying to brush him off.

"No, it was Tetsutsun, wasn't it?" he said with a smirk.

It irritated her that he knew so much, and with a woman's jealousy, she wondered whether the children preferred him to her.

"Well, I don't want to talk about that."

"Yes, I understand," he answered, backing down.

"I was wondering if you've ever heard of the 'fly's dance'?"

"The 'fly's dance'?"

"Yes, as in a fly that dances."

"No way."

He didn't seem to believe her, thank goodness, which meant that the children had left him in the dark.

"Go catch me a live one, and I'll make him dance for you."

"You're putting me on, aren't you?"

He was still suspicious, but he headed into the bathroom and soon returned with a large bluish-black fly.

"The bigger, the better," said Ms. Kotani, pleased.

She braced herself, but the thought of touching the thing made her cringe. Even so, she was determined to surprise this annoyingly provoking man. She thought she was going to die, but she performed the operation as Isao had shown her, being sure to shield what she was doing from Mr. Adachi.

"There," she said, placing the fly on the desk. It didn't move at first, but when she banged the desk, it confusedly began to dance.

"Oooh!" screamed Mr. Adachi hysterically.

The reaction thoroughly satisfied her.

"Hey, look at this!" he yelled, to no one in particular. "A fly's dancing! Hurry! Come here!"

The other teachers ambled over and gazed in wonder at the dancing fly.

"How did you do that?"

"Should I fill you in?" began Ms. Kotani, who was feeling more and more proud of herself. "Well, in taxonomy, flies are classified in the group of insects called Diptera, which means that just like mosquitoes and horseflies, they're characterized by having two wings. But it seems that long, long ago, flies used to have four wings, just like butterflies and dragonflies, and the vestigial remains of those bottom wings are still present. The degenerate wing is called a halter or balancer, and it controls the fly's sense of balance when it's flying. So if you pull them off, the fly can't fly anymore, and if it tries, it just looks like it's dancing."

"Wow! You sound like a real authority!"

The teachers were in such awe that Ms. Kotani burst out laughing.

"It's all explained in those books I was just reading."

After she came clean, it all became something of a joke, but even still, everyone was impressed. When the small commotion died down, and she was left alone with Mr. Adachi, she filled him in on the rest.

"The fact is, I learned about that from Tetsuzo."

"He knows about something so difficult?" Mr. Adachi asked in disbelief.

"Well, not really, but I guess he learned from experience that if you pull off the thread-like things under the wings, the fly gets like that. He showed the kids at the disposal plant, and Isao showed me."

"Wow, that's quite a story! I guess that means that Tetsuzo's quite a scientist, doesn't it?"

"That's right. And on top of that, I read something that really got to me. I copied it down, and I'd like you to read it."

She handed him the paper, which read: "After their parents bring them into the world, flies spend their entire lives alone—without friends, without families, and without homes. They live in constant fear of bees, spiders, birds, and other predators, but they themselves prey on nothing, feeding instead on the refuse of society. It is neither a heroic life, nor a cruel one; rather, it is an extremely modest life, like that of the common people."

Mr. Adachi broke out laughing when he finished reading.

"What's this? It sounds just like Tetsuzo."

"It does, doesn't it? So you think so, too?"

"Yes, I do. He's tried to live modestly, but people keep cutting in. What's more, the ones cutting in are teachers."

"Yes, and there's one more thing that bothered me. In one of the books I read, it said that when flies first become active in the early spring, they spend their time outside, sipping nectar from flowers or sap from trees. They only move on to trash, excrement, and rotting food when it gets warmer. But if that's the case, the flies aren't the bad ones. The bad ones are the human beings who put out their trash and rotting food when it gets warm. You don't have to side with the flies that far, but you do have to admit that since Tetsuzo starts raising his flies in the spring and then breeds those flies, the criticism that his flies are covered with germs is incorrect."

"I see what you mean."

"I didn't give it much thought before, but I heard that the only flies Tetsuzo won't raise are houseflies. Apparently, his reason is that they feed on excrement. Well, that makes a lot of sense."

"Wow."

"I guess I've made a lot of mistakes with him because I misunderstood him."

"You're not the only one."

"Well, if you don't mind, I'd like you to go to Tetsuzo's house with me."

"Why?"

"I might get scratched again."

Mr. Adachi laughed.

"What are we coming to," he chided her, "when teachers are scared of their students?"

"But I, uh . . . ," she said, on the verge of tears.

"Okay, okay," he said, standing up. "You're still a new teacher, so you win."

When they showed up at the disposal plant, the children came running up at full speed and started jumping up on Mr. Adachi like grasshoppers. Only Jun, looking somewhat self-conscious, swung from Ms. Kotani's hand.

"It's Adachi!" one of them yelled.

Shigeko, Keiko, Misae, and some others—who had not appeared for Ms. Kotani—came running up, too. Keiko was Isao's little sister, and Misae was Jun's.

"Hey, Tokuji, how's Kintaro doin'?" asked Mr. Adachi. He really seemed to know about everything.

"I'm training 'im right now."

"He's a lot of work, isn't he?"

"He sure is."

"Your mother used to say the same about you."

"Shucks!" said Tokuji, scratching his head.

"Can I have a hug?" asked Misae. Dressed in a plain shimmy, she put out her arms.

"There you are," said Mr. Adachi, pulling her into his arms. Misae was one of his students.

"Stop actin' like a baby," said Jun, poking his sister in the back.

"Stop it," whined Misae. Ms. Kotani thought she was very cute.

"Is this how it is during class?" she asked Mr. Adachi.

What with Kimi climbing up on his shoulders and Misae hugging him, she couldn't imagine what his classes might be like.

"Yeh, it's usually something like this."

"Would you mind if I sat in on one some time?"

"Sure, drop by anytime."

By the time Misae finally let go, Mr. Adachi's shirt was covered with sweat, but he didn't seem to mind.

Tetsuzo was giving Lucky a bath in the backyard, and when the group arrived, Lucky stared at them with a pleading look, his body covered with bubbles.

"Ever since ya gave Tetsutsun that bath," Jun whispered to Ms. Kotani, "he's been givin' Lucky baths, too. I think he's copyin' ya."

"Really?" said Ms. Kotani, beaming with delight.

"No, not like that, Tetsutsun," said Mr. Adachi, jumping in and giving him a hand. "Dogs hate it when they get water in their ears. Hold his ears down like this when you wash him. Yeh, that's right."

He assisted with the chore as if he were doing it for himself, and Ms. Kotani couldn't help thinking that he was the most laid back person in the world. That was probably why some people criticized him for being a bit rough around the edges.

With two people washing him, Lucky was finished with his bath in no time.

"Look at that!" said Mr. Adachi. "He's clean as a whistle!"

Lucky tilted his head and stared at him with a confused look.

"Tetsutsun, could you show me your little friends now?" asked Mr. Adachi.

He was looking at the bottles of flies before he even finished asking. Tetsuzo held himself stiff, obviously on his guard.

"Wow! This one's pretty neat, too! So how many different kinds have you got?"

Mr. Adachi started counting.

"Hey, Tetsutsun, get over here!"

In a flash, he hugged Tetsuzo from behind and plopped him down in his lap.

"So what are these little ones called?"

Tetsuzo squirmed.

"Tetsutsun only knows the names of four flies," said Isao. "He knows all kinds of stuff about 'em, but unless ya tell 'im what they're called, he doesn't know. He's completely clueless."

"That's right," said Jun, picking up for his friend. "And he only knows those four names 'cause me and Isao checked it out for 'im. By the way, that ragged old guidebook at school is useless. Hurry up and buy us a new one."

"And since he don't know what they're called," Isao continued, "he just makes up the names himself. Those little flies there are always scuttlin' around, so I guess that's why he calls 'em 'scuttle flies.'"

"Mr. Adachi," said Ms. Kotani, in shock. "There's nothing made up about that. It's the common name for them. Look, some of them don't have wings, right? Well, in some species of scuttle flies, the females don't have wings."

"Wow! Tetsutsun, I can't believe you! They're really called 'scuttle flies.'"

Tetsuzo didn't say a word.

Ms. Kotani pulled out the book she had found on the classification of flies.

"Tetsutsun," said Mr. Adachi, smiling. "Ms. Kotani wants to learn more about flies, and she'd like to be your student. I hope you'll be willing to teach her."

Looking back and forth between the flies and the book, they discovered the names of nine different species: the housefly, the false stable fly, the little housefly, the blowfly, the Caesar green bottle fly, the green bottle fly, the flesh fly, the scuttle fly, and the fruit fly. Tetsuzo wasn't raising any houseflies, but they were so common that everyone could identify them.

Only one species remained unidentified, and since Tetsuzo had only six of them, it obviously was a rare one. The children pressed in close, in spite of the heat, and flipped through the pages.

"It's this one!" a voice burst out.

"Huh?"

Astounded, Ms. Kotani stared at Tetsuzo's face.

"It's this one," he said again, and she looked to where he was pointing. It read, "*Chrysomya Pinguis*."

It was the first time she had ever heard him speak.

7. Playing Beggar

Tetsuzo spoke. He finally spoke. Ms. Kotani was so happy that she nearly burst out laughing several times on the train home from school. She and her husband worked, so she usually had to stop off at the supermarket on the way home. That evening, she was on cloud nine as she did the shopping, and at the checkout, she nearly walked off without receiving her change. When the teller laughed at her, she only thought how people take pleasure in the strangest things.

When she got home, her husband was waiting for her.

"Your dad called a little while ago," he said. "They finished with the formalities on the land, and he wants you to come over and pick up the paperwork."

"I see."

"That means we'll be able to build our own house soon," he said, quite pleased.

Ms. Kotani's father was the last of several generations of doctors, and the family had accumulated a small amount of property. Her parents expected her to support herself and discouraged her from looking for any financial assistance, but since land prices had drastically increased, they figured that purchasing land would be impossible for a young couple and decided to partition up some of the land for their daughter.

"I've got some good news, too," she said.

When she told her husband about what happened with

Tetsuzo, he looked bewildered. He must have thought it odd to put such news in the same category as his. That evening, Ms. Kotani and her husband were in a good mood for the first time in a long time. If only such evenings could last forever.

During September, schools throughout Japan prepare for their athletic meets, and since teachers and students are usually exhausted, it was a time ripe for accidents. Himematsu Elementary School was no exception and experienced three traffic accidents in a row.

Ms. Kotani's class had a couple of unpleasant incidents, too.

The first happened during lunchtime recess.

Shortly after eating lunch with her students and returning to the teachers' room, Ms. Kotani realized that she had forgotten something and headed back to the classroom. A dozen or so students were still there, screaming and yelling at the back of the room, so she checked to see what the commotion was about.

Satoshi was kneeling on the floor with a handkerchief spread out in front of him, and the other children were lined up in a row facing him. The child at the front of the line tossed something onto the handkerchief.

"Thank you oh so very much," said Satoshi, bowing his head low and hiding the object behind his back. The children shrieked with laughter, and the girl who was next in line stepped forward.

"Here you are, Mr. Beggar," she said, placing a white object on the handkerchief.

"Thank you oh so very much," Satoshi said again, with another bow.

"What a poor little beggar," said the next girl, as if they were playing house. "But don't forget to beg."

With a smirk on his face, Satoshi did as he was told: he put out his hands and begged. Ms. Kotani had moved a little closer, and this time she could see what was placed in his hands. It was a slice of bread.

"What are you doing!" she yelled, in a sharper tone than intended. Satoshi scurried to hide the objects he had collected.

"Satoshi, let me see what you have there."

Reluctantly, he handed over the fourteen or fifteen slices of bread that he had hidden.

Ms. Kotani was furious.

"Who started this game? Huh? Answer me, Terue!"

"I don't know," the girl answered on the verge of tears. "Everybody else was playing, so I played, too."

"And Satoshi, you're no less to blame than they are! Pretending to be a beggar! You ought to be ashamed of yourself!"

Ms. Kotani found the smirk on Satoshi's face to be especially annoying. When she questioned the other children, she discovered that the game had been going on for four or five days now and that Satoshi had taken home nearly twenty slices of bread each time.

Since her visit with Mr. Adachi to see Satoshi's sister, Kimi,

Ms. Kotani had been keeping a close eye on him, but she hadn't noticed anything to suggest that things had gotten so bad that he would need to take bread home from school.

She consulted with Mr. Adachi.

"I don't know what to think myself," he said. "Why don't we go out there and see what's going on?"

Ms. Kotani had other plans, so she asked him to go on his own. The next day, he reported on his visit.

"Satoshi says he didn't have any special reason for doing it. He admitted to taking a lot of bread home with him, but after he ate four or five slices, he threw the rest away. I was worried he might be trying to sell them to a bakery or something, but it was petty of me to suspect him."

Mr. Adachi paused and scratched his head.

"But, you know, I think I can understand how he feels. Certainly, it was a waste, but I bet all that bread gave him a sense of security. Even if his father didn't show up for two or three days, he'd be able to get by if he had so much bread to eat. He probably felt relieved knowing he had enough to throw away at the end of each day. Or do you think I'm overanalyzing everything?"

Ms. Kotani was silent.

"And one other thing. You said you were annoyed by that smirk on his face. Well, I think you're wrong there. I'm sure he felt so humiliated that he couldn't have done it without smirking."

She could say nothing in reply.

The second disagreeable incident occurred the next day, shortly after music class.

Ms. Kotani was heading back to the classroom after returning the instruments to the music room. Curiously, a group of students were standing around Tetsuzo in the hallway singing, and as she passed by, her only thought was that it was the song they had just practiced during class. She smiled at them and started to head into the classroom, but her feet unconsciously came to a halt. She was only half-listening, so it almost didn't register, but something about the song wasn't right. Certainly, it had the same melody, but the lyrics had been changed.

Buzz, buzz, buzz, look at all the flies
All around Usui
Gold and silver flies
Buzz, buzz, buzz, look at all the flies

Usui was Tetsuzo's family name.

Ms. Kotani hit the roof.

"Knock it off!" she yelled, her body shaking. She wanted to say more, but she was speechless with anger. If she had been one to hit students, she would have hit them.

What kind of children would act like this? First, there was the incident with Satoshi, and then this. It was as if they were devoid of all human feeling and didn't possess a shred of kindness or consideration. They barely seemed human.

"Why, you kids!" she burst out in frustration.

Her voice became choked with emotion, and water came to her eyes. Through the tears, she glared at them for what seemed like ages.

Late that night, after taking a long bath, Ms. Kotani sat down in front of the mirror and gazed at her reflection. She looked tired and pathetic, and even had bags under her eyes. It was hard to believe that she was only twenty-two years old.

That evening, she had had another quarrel with her husband. He had invited over an architect friend, who was going to draw up the blueprints for their new house, and when they were discussing the layout, she just couldn't get excited.

"Don't you think that was rude?" he yelled when they were alone again. "He came out here for our benefit, and even though you're the main person in all this, you couldn't even give him a decent answer."

"I'm sorry," she apologized meekly. "I just couldn't get into it for some reason or other. I guess it doesn't seem all that important anymore."

"Not important! What the hell is that supposed to mean!" he screamed, even angrier than before.

"I know it's unfair of me, but that's how I was feeling. Let's just forget it," she said.

Late that night, she gazed at her gently snoring husband and apologized to him in her heart. Ever since they had gotten married, she had been unkind to him, and she felt like a naughty little girl.

The next day was Sunday, and her husband had to work, so Ms. Kotani decided to take a trip to Nara. When she was in college, she had been a member of the Ancient Japanese Art Club and had visited many temples in Kyoto and Nara, but she hadn't visited any since getting married. As a wife and teacher, she knew that that was unavoidable, but even so, she missed her temple visits.

She changed trains at Tsuruhashi and got off at Saidaiji Station. A large modern building stood in front of the station, and as she stared at it, she recalled the words of her college teacher.

"Back when I was a student," he had grumbled, "this was a rustic country station. When you got off the train, you had to jump over a rotten old wooden fence. There was a narrow dirt road and a stream, and other than that, nothing but stretches of rice fields. As soon as you came out of the station, the smell of the temple's earthen walls would lap up against you."

Ms. Kotani loved Saidaiji Temple. Not only was it her first temple, but after visiting dozens of others, it was also her favorite.

After turning the corner at the phone booth, she could see the dear old earthen walls. Saidaiji's walls were really nice. They were discolored a yellowish brown like a persimmon and sections had started to crumble. The rain had worn the wall down to give it some unevenness. The effect was much more soothing than a shiny new wall. She passed through the old temple gate to the white pebble path. If you walked with firm and steady steps, you could almost hear the stones murmuring to you.

Saidaiji's bamboo was also nice. Inside the temple grounds was a narrow path, concealed in a grove of bamboo. The old white walls, which still remained, harmonized nicely with the bamboo's green. If you took a deep breath, you could feel the green sink into you all the way down to your fingernails.

The inside of the main temple was pleasantly cool even during the summer. You just had to go barefoot. Ms. Kotani took off her shoes and socks, and came in touch with the coolness. She walked towards the left, where the statue of the Bodhisattva Zenzai Doji was housed.

"Hello," she said to the statue with a smile. "Thanks for waiting for me."

The eyes of Zenzai Doji were as beautiful as ever. More like the eyes of a rabbit than a human being, they were overflowing with a quiet and radiant kindness, as if deep in prayer, or reflecting on life. She sighed, and gazed at the statue for a long time.

"I'm glad I've come," she murmured with a sense of relief.

The lobby of the temple was cool and spacious, and sometimes people wandered around there, lost in thought. Ms. Kotani sat down. No one was there today. The front gate and the remains of the old five-storied pagoda were surrounded with greenery and looked refreshing.

"Why are you so beautiful?"

The image of Zenzai Doji burned vividly in her eyes.

"You're too beautiful. But why?"

Ms. Kotani couldn't understand it.

Suddenly, for no apparent reason, she recalled the words of one of her high school teachers. Many students used to make fun of him, saying that he was a Tokyo University geek. They made jokes about his unimpressive appearance and about how he used to jiggle his leg nervously as he ate his customary lunch of plain *udon* noodles. Many would brazenly cheat on his tests or talk to their friends right in front of him during class.

But Ms. Kotani could never make fun of him.

One day, in the middle of class, he made a dramatic pause, and said, "Human beings must resist. That's right, resistance is what is most important. Ladies and gentlemen, please remember: for human beings to be beautiful, they must never forget the spirit of resistance."

Everyone in the class was struck dumb, and Ms. Kotani didn't have a clue either. She had completely forgotten the incident. Until now.

"For human beings to be beautiful," she murmured to herself, "they must resist."

The words startled her. She thought of Tetsuzo, Satoshi, and the other children that lived at the disposal plant. And she thought of Mr. Adachi, too. She had asked Zenzai Doji why he was so beautiful, but she might have asked the same question in a different way: why wasn't she beautiful? And why weren't the children teasing Tetsuzo beautiful?

She thought of the kindness of the disposal plant children. She thought of Tetsuzo's strength of will in raising his flies. She thought of the determination of Satoshi in bringing home bread. And she thought of herself.

Turning pale, she stood up, and the merciless screeching of the cicadas stung her from behind.

8. Bad Guys

"Open your books to page six," said Mr. Adachi in a booming voice.

The students opened their Arts and Crafts textbooks to a children's picture of red crabs lined up in a row. A heading at the top of the page read, "Lining up Animals."

"So what do you think of this one?" asked Mr. Adachi.

"It's crappy!" many of the students called out.

Ms. Kotani, who was observing the class from the back of the room, was shocked. What could be the point of getting students to criticize the model picture in the textbook?

"What's crappy about it?" Mr. Adachi continued.

About half the students raised their hands.

"Okay, Haruko," he said, calling on a student.

"It's crappy 'cause they're all the same," she said.

"Could you be a bit more specific?"

"They're all the same shape and the same color. It's boring."

"Okay, roger that," said Mr. Adachi, pointing to the next student.

"Crabs are living things, right? But these crabs're all lined up straight, kinda like apples or oranges or something. It's weird. They oughta be crawlin' all over the place."

"Roger that," said Mr. Adachi. You couldn't tell whether he agreed with the boy or not. He just continued having one student speak after another. Ms. Kotani was impressed: second-graders were actually speaking out critically.

"Well, you all seem to know what you're talking about," Mr. Adachi concluded, "so I guess I can go ahead and take a nap."

The students started yelling in protest.

"No way!"

"No fair!"

"You get paid every month," called out a student in the front, "so teach like you're supposed to!"

Everyone laughed, and the atmosphere became even more friendly and relaxed. Mr. Adachi truly had a special talent for unlocking children's hearts.

He asked three children to go to the blackboard and draw one crab each.

"Okay," he said when they were finished, "who can draw a crab that's different from these?"

Students were sent to the board in groups of four or five, and before long, the entire blackboard was covered with pictures of crabs. Every single one was different. The picture in the textbook did indeed pale by comparison.

"Anyone can draw a good crab as long as they don't imitate," said Mr. Adachi, erasing the board. "There are all kinds of crabs: fat ones, skinny ones, spoiled ones that always run to their mom or dad for a hug, ones that are always getting into fights, and ones that get caught sneaking food out of the refrigerator."

The students began to grin in embarrassment when they realized that he was talking about them.

"You can draw any kind of crab you want, but you have to explain to me what he's doing. That's our agreement for today's picture."

The students also gave good opinions when they were discussing how to arrange the crabs. One student suggested arranging them in a spiral, but Mr. Adachi criticized that as being too conventional. Another student suggested arranging them so that it would look like a circus or a sumo tournament when viewed from above. Their way of talking was rough, but everyone in the class was lively and active. Mr. Adachi was his regular self.

Ms. Kotani had been wondering how clingy behavior, such as Kimi's climbing up on his shoulders, would be acted out in the classroom, and when the students started working on their pictures, she soon had the answer to her question.

Most students worked independently, but a few brought their pictures to Mr. Adachi and tried to get him to help.

"Is this okay?" they would ask.

"Decide for yourself if it's okay or not," he would answer coldly. "It's your picture, isn't it?"

He obviously kept in mind that there were times to discourage dependency. Another student brought up his picture, and Ms. Kotani watched closely to see if he would be driven away, too.

"I'm thinking of havin' my crab blowin' light blue and white bubbles. What'd ya think of that?" the student asked.

"That's a great idea," Mr. Adachi answered kindly. "I think it'd be cool if you drew 'em as small as you can." As long as students had ideas of their own, he gladly gave them advice.

Ms. Kotani's class was watching a movie that lasted for two periods, so she decided to stay and observe Mr. Adachi's composition class, too. The subject seemed to be giving a lot of teachers trouble, for nearly a dozen stood in the back to observe, and Mr. Orihashi and Mr. Ota were diligently taking notes. Even with the crowd at the back of the room, Mr. Adachi's students were as composed and relaxed as always.

"Today, I'm gonna give you extra special service," said Mr. Adachi, sounding like a shopkeeper at the market. "I'm gonna show you how to write a well written composition in one shot, without going to any trouble at all."

"You're lyin'! You're always goin' on about how much trouble we should take!"

Mr. Adachi's students didn't pull any punches.

"That's why I'm callin' it 'extra special' service."

"Oh, you're just sayin' that 'cause there's other teachers watchin'."

"What're ya talking about? They're nothin' but a bunch of boogers. They got nothin' to do with us."

The students laughed to hear Ms. Kotani and the other teachers dismissed as boogers, but then they felt sorry for them, and glanced to the back of the room. The teachers smiled wryly.

"And so, without further ado," said Mr. Adachi, speaking like a circus performer. "I present to you today, as the result of my many years of strenuous effort, the great method that I have invented. To tell the truth, I'd prefer not to give away my secret, but you guys are so darn cute that I've decided to swallow my tears and fill you in. If you can whip out a good composition, you can also tell if one's well-written, so you're really getting two methods for the price of one—and what's more, it's free. You guys sure are lucky, aren't you?"

Mr. Adachi's students might have been strong-minded, but they were still second-graders, and most of them listened with their mouths hanging open, completely caught up in their teacher's speech. Every teacher has had the experience of not getting anything done because they have to constantly warn students about talking or not paying attention, but in Mr. Adachi's class, such problems didn't exist.

"In every composition, there are good guys and bad guys. If you can distinguish them, and then get rid of the bad guys, you'll soon have a good composition. Pretty easy, ain't it?"

Mr. Adachi passed out a one-page handout.

"Kenji, could you read the first composition?"

"'At seven o'clock, I woke up. Everyday, I practice for the athletic meet. Today I went shopping with my mother. My father came home at eight thirty. I watched some TV and went to bed.'"

When he finished reading, everyone burst out laughing. They could tell that it was a horrible composition.

"Akira, read the next one."

"'On my way home from school, I saw a bulldozer. It was moving around and making lots of noise. I just had to watch. I was thinking if he ran over me, I'd be flattened like a pancake. It stopped moving, so I figured I'd go home. The street was real hot. That was kind of strange 'cause there wasn't any electric cord or anything.'"

"So now, finally," said Mr. Adachi, "I'm gonna tell you about the good guys and the bad guys, so scrape the dirt out of your ears, and listen closely."

He wrote on the blackboard:

—things done

—things seen

—things felt

—things thought

—things said

—things heard

—other

Then he drew an X next to "things done," and put a check mark next to everything else.

"Mr. Adachi, 'things done' are bad guys?" asked one student, unable to wait.

"You got it," said Mr. Adachi, with perfect nonchalance. "So now let's take a closer look at that essay you guys just laughed at. 'At seven o'clock, I woke up.' Is this something done, something seen, or something thought?"

"Something done!" the students answered in unison.

"Well then, it's a bad guy. Mark that sentence with an X."

The students were thrilled to draw X's on their handouts.

"Next is 'Everyday, I practice for the athletic meet.' How about this one?"

"It's something done, so it's a bad guy."

"Well, we can mark that one with an X, too."

"'Today I went shopping with my mother.'"

"It's a bad guy! It's a bad guy!" screamed the students, before Mr. Adachi had even asked them.

Eventually, every sentence had been marked with an X, which deeply impressed the students.

"You said if we got rid of all the bad guys, we'd have a good composition, but if we get rid of all the bad guys in this one, there won't be anything left at all!"

"You got it. No matter how many of these kinds of sentences you write, you're gonna end up with nothing. So if that's all you're going to write, you're better off just taking a nap."

The students roared with laughter.

The second composition received check marks for every sentence, and Kazuo, the student who wrote it, broke out smiling. He had been scared to death that his composition wasn't very good.

"At this point, I want to tell you something very important. In the real world, there are good guys and bad guys, and if there aren't any bad guys, the good guys won't stand out. Compositions are the same: if you only have good guys, it's boring, but if you put in a few bad guys, it'll be more interesting."

Mr. Adachi made an important point: if the students mindlessly eliminated all sentences about "things done," their composition might end up being awkward. He had anticipated this problem and urged them to be careful.

"In compositions, it's possible to distinguish good guys from bad guys, but with human beings, it's not so easy. Sometimes, someone you think is a good guy turns out to be a bad guy. And sometimes, someone that's labeled a bad guy turns out to be a good guy."

He seemed to be directing his sarcasm towards the teachers at the back of the room, and Mr. Orihashi chuckled.

After class, Mr. Adachi returned to the teachers' room, where he was thanked for his trouble and brought some tea.

"I don't need any of that crap," he said, pulling a black bottle out of his desk.

"Don't do that," said the teacher sitting next to him. As she kept an eye out for the Assistant Principal, she poked him in the ribs.

"Just a nip," said Mr. Adachi, and making a face like a baby, he took a swig of the offensive liquid.

You really couldn't tell whether he was a good guy or a bad guy.

"Mr. Adachi, that was indeed a most memorable class," said Ms. Sachiko Kimura, who was nicknamed the Queen of Praise. "I really learned a lot."

"Did you really?" he asked, poking fun at her. He disliked her because although she was quick to praise, she rarely put in any effort of her own.

"Yes, I really learned a lot. Thank you very much."

Ms. Kotani expressed her appreciation, too.

"No problem," he said in return, his face beaming. He was not past showing some favoritism.

"But I'm not going to copy you."

"Of course not," he answered with a smile. Most teachers would say that they were going to use his ideas or that they would appreciate his help, but Mr. Adachi was fed up with teachers like that.

"Even if I'm having a tough time, I'll figure it out for myself, and come up with my own lessons."

"Absolutely," his said, his smile broadening. He could tell that she had become a different kind of teacher.

"Ms. Kotani."

"Huh?" said Ms. Kotani, turning back to him again.

"You look really pretty today."

"Don't be such an idiot," she said, and then she reddened at having spoken roughly.

She had become a lot like him.

9. The Crow's Treasure

On this particular day, Ms. Kotani visited Satoshi's house and then stopped off to see Tetsuzo. Instead of taking the first train home after school, she had gotten into the habit of visiting the homes of three or four students, the last of whom was always Tetsuzo. As a result, she was usually an hour or two late in getting home, which annoyed her husband.

"Do teachers really have to do all that?" he had asked.

"I'm not doing it because I have to," she answered. "I'm doing it because it's interesting."

Her husband stared at her in disbelief.

Ms. Kotani's visits allowed her to witness various occupations in action, and she availed herself of the opportunity to experience them firsthand. At a bakery, she was allowed to make bread, and at a butcher's shop, she learned how to carve up meat and evaluate various cuts for purchasing. She also learned about salvaging and other kinds of work. One set of parents even had her arbitrate one of their arguments, which made her keenly aware of how people had different attitudes towards the same things.

As she learned about the work and lives of so many people, she came to feel that her own life was insignificant and pathetic. Her childhood had been uneventful, and she had gotten married for no particular reason. She tried to talk to her husband about all this, but he couldn't understand. "Oh, never mind," she finally told him. "Let's just see who can live more fully. See if you can give me a run for my money." Her young husband had stared at her in bewilderment.

Ms. Kotani circled around to the back of the house.

"Tetsuzo!" she called.

Lucky, who had grown quite attached to her, came bounding out of nowhere. As he frolicked around her, Tetsuzo came trudging out of the house.

"Anything new with your little friends?"

Ms. Kotani examined the fly bottles, which had been carefully labeled with the names of the various species. Some labels were obviously done by Ms. Kotani, but Tetsuzo had done the others. The labels made them look even more like specimen bottles, and Ms. Kotani thought they looked quite impressive.

"Did you practice?" she asked.

"Uh," Tetsuzo answered.

He had continued to grunt incomprehensibly, but Ms. Kotani no longer let it bother her. She walked into the house without knocking and opened his notebook. Atrocious handwriting is sometimes compared to wriggling worms, but in Tetsuzo's case that would be an understatement. The worms had writhed and twisted until they fainted dead away, so that only he or Ms. Kotani could possibly decode their meaning.

Ms. Kotani had prepared about twenty cards on which she had written the names of various flies. On days when Ms. Kotani couldn't make it, Tetsuzo would study on his own by copying the cards into his notebook, but on days like today, when they were together, he learned by playing a *karuta* card game. Ms. Kotani would read one of the cards aloud, and Tetsuzo would try to grab it as quickly as possible.

"Shall we get started, Tetsuzo?" she asked, laying the cards out in front of him.

"'*Chrysomya Pinguis*,'" she read.

Tetsuzo grabbed the card immediately. It was the fly he had identified from Ms. Kotani's book and the first one he had remembered.

"'Blue bottle fly.'"

He picked that one up after a short pause.

"'Cheese fly.'"

That one didn't take him long either. Not surprisingly, Tetsuzo had an easier time with the shorter names.

"'Little housefly.'"

That one took him a very long time.

"'*Lutescens* fruit fly.'"

He couldn't get that one at all. Species of fruit flies tended to have long names, so he had a hard time with them.

"It's this one," she told him.

Whenever she had to point one out for him, his face contorted into an indescribably complicated expression of frustration, shame, and embarrassment.

"It's okay," she said, patting him on the head. "Just take your time and learn them when you can. Okay, let's try the next one. 'Scuttle fly.'"

Tetsuzo searched with all his might.

Ms. Kotani never imagined that Tetsuzo's flies would come in so handy. When he was in school, he never did anything: he did not open his textbook, write in his notebook, or play with his classmates. He might have been living and breathing, but he was no more than a vegetable.

But the flies got Tetsuzo started on learning his letters, and that wasn't all. They also got him started drawing pictures. When Ms. Kotani told him that the library book on flies was due, he started copying out the fly illustrations that very evening. She felt sorry for him, so she ordered the book from a publisher in Tokyo as a present. After that, he started working on detailed illustrations.

It is said that a person's intelligence is revealed through his drawings, and Tetsuzo's pictures didn't look at all like ones drawn by a first-grader. The shapes were sometimes a bit distorted, but even extremely trivial details were drawn correctly. For example, he paid careful attention to the veins running along the fly's wings. In houseflies, the fourth vein (counting from the head, the fifth line running along the inside part of the wing) is bent like a V and connects to the third vein. In other flies, the fourth vein runs parallel to the third vein or is only slightly bent. Incredibly, Tetsuzo correctly made such detailed distinctions in his pictures. Ms. Kotani had to confess that she had been beginning to wonder whether he was mentally handicapped, but when she saw his pictures, she knew that that was not the case.

After he received the book, the number of species Tetsuzo was raising suddenly increased. Cabbage flies and blue bottle flies are extremely rare, but he found some at a food processing shop and began carefully breeding them himself.

"Okay, Tetsuzo, next we're going to practice our writing. How many labels do you think you'll be able to replace today?"

Ms. Kotani had initially written all of the labels because Tetsuzo's handwriting was illegible, but as his writing improved, they began replacing her labels with his. She was looking forward to the day when he would be able to replace all of her labels with his own.

Human talent truly was mysterious. Tetsuzo could draw fly diagrams with great precision, but he could only write his letters after much practice—just like ordinary children. Passion seemed to be the essential ingredient that allowed you to vastly exceed your limitations. Mr. Adachi had said that he was full of treasure, and now she knew what he meant. As she watched Tetsuzo intent on his work, she secretly wondered what new treasures he had in store for her.

Isao and his friends were tired of playing and came over to Tetsuzo's house for a break.

"Hey, there," said Shiro, when he saw Ms. Kotani.

"Hey, yourself," she replied casually.

The children noisily trooped into the house and gathered around Tetsuzo and his teacher.

"Wow, ya got a tutor for free, huh?" said Isao, poking Tetsuzo in the ribs.

"Knock it off!" said Ms. Kotani, with a stern expression. "We're in the middle of work, so don't get in the way!"

Tetsuzo took no notice and went right on practicing his letters. Noise and excitement didn't faze him in the least.

"Ms. Kotani," said Isao.

"Huh?"

"It'd be cool if Tetsutsun learned his letters and wrote a paper on flies or something."

"Yes, and since he'd be a professor, you could carry his briefcase."

"Me? Carry Tetsutsun's briefcase? Don't make me laugh. Huh, Tetsutsun?" Isao smacked Tetsuzo on the butt and fell down laughing.

"Where's Jun?" asked Ms. Kotani. "Is something wrong?"

"Misae's in bed with a fever, so he's home taking care of 'er."

"Misae's sick?"

"Yeh, her face is all red, and she's having trouble breathin'."

"That sounds pretty bad. I think I'll pay her a visit."

After telling Tetsuzo to keep working, Ms. Kotani left with the children to see Misae. Most of the mothers in the neighborhood had to work, so the disposal plant children were accustomed to just walking into people's homes during the day, and Ms. Kotani did the same.

"How are you feeling, honey?"

"I got a fever of 102."

Misae had a cold towel on her forehead and looked washed out, but she gave Ms. Kotani a little smile for having come.

"Jun, I'm impressed."

Jun sat on the floor with his knees in his arms and a washbasin in front of him.

"I can't play," he complained.

Ms. Kotani noticed that chewing gum, marbles, stickers, some fancy colored paper, and various other objects had been placed next to Misae's pillow.

"Are these get-well presents?" she asked.

"Yeh, Isao and everybody gave 'em to me."

There was also a liquor bottle lid, a rubber snake, and a broken watchband.

"Are these presents, too?"

Standing off to the side, Isao and his friends looked away in embarrassment.

"I'm going to get you something, too. What would you like, Misae?"

"Ice cream."

"Idiot," said Jun. "You got sick from eatin' too much ice cream."

"I don't think you should have ice cream while you're sick, honey. But I'll get you something good, okay?"

Ms. Kotani went off with the children to look for Misae's present.

"I wonder what should I get her?"

She wandered around the shopping district, and the children tagged along after her.

"I got a slight fever," said Takeo in a babyish voice, "so get *me* something, too."

The other children chewed him out.

In the end, Ms. Kotani settled on some small flowers that looked like lilies and a hexagonal Japanese paper box filled with chocolate. She didn't think they were very interesting.

"The presents you guys got are much better. Mine look pathetic next to yours."

The children were totally perplexed.

"I just bought her something with money, but you gave her something that you valued. Yours are much more heartfelt and sincere."

"I'd rather have chocolate than sincerity," candidly admitted Yoshikichi.

As they were talking, it came to light that each of the children owned something that they valued.

"I wish you'd show them to me," requested Ms. Kotani.

"We'd be happy to!" they screamed, their eyes gleaming. And they raced off to retrieve their treasures.

Ms. Kotani was handing Misae her get-well present when Isao returned first with a big box in his arms. She didn't know for sure, but they looked like the broken parts of various machines, including a radio and a clock.

"I can make an engine out of all this," he said proudly, and he quickly assembled the scattered pieces of metal. Ms. Kotani gazed in wonder at his creation.

"This would be neat when we're doing sketches for art class. Could you lend it to me some time?"

"Sure, I'd be happy to."

One by one, the children returned with various objects. Though all of them were junk, many were also quite intriguing.

"Keiko, what are those?"

"What'd ya think they are?" put in Isao. "Take a guess."

They were obviously made of glass, but they had various shapes and colors. There were pink ones, which were pretty and shiny, and somber blue ones, which looked like pieces of pottery. Keiko had a lot of the blue ones.

"They're very pretty, but I have no idea. I give up, so what are they?"

"They're made from melted bottles. Sometimes bottles get mixed in with the other garbage and burned by mistake. And when they're burned for a long time, this is how they turn out. They're mixed in with the ash."

"Wow," said Ms. Kotani, impressed again.

"Do ya want one?"

"But they mean a lot to you, don't they?"

"If ya want one, I'll give ya one."

"Okay, I want one."

"Well, then, go ahead and take one."

Ms. Kotani picked a bright-green stone from the pile.

Koji collected Styrofoam, which he used to make various kinds of robots.

"Koji, these are really neat. Why didn't you enter them in the school art exhibit?"

The robots made Koji's worth clear, and Ms. Kotani couldn't help feeling regret that Ms. Murano felt the way she did.

Staring at all the junk the children had collected, Ms. Kotani recalled what people said about the crow's treasure. Crows have the habit of collecting useless objects, and they'll carry almost anything into their nests: popped balloons, shoelaces, and other bric-a-brac. As far as collecting things went, the disposal plant children were a lot like crows, but Ms. Kotani felt that by saving things, they had mastered the spirit of making use of all that had been thrown away.

10. Mr. Baku

"Sorry about that," said Ms. Kotani upon her return.

Tetsuzo was silently practicing his letters in the dim room.

"Boy, you really wrote a lot of them. 'Flesh fly' and 'little house fly' look pretty nice, don't they? Today we'll be able to put on two new labels."

Ms. Kotani cut a long, narrow strip of paper for him.

"Okay, let's do a nice copy. Watch what you're doing and be very careful."

Tetsuzo wrote out the names of the flies as best he could.

A short time later, as they were putting on the new labels, Mr. Baku came home from work.

"Ms. Kotani," he said, as soon as he saw her, "if you don't mind, I have a favor to ask you."

"What is it, Mr. Baku?"

"I know it's a bit rude to ask so suddenly, but would you stay and have dinner with us tonight?"

Her husband's angry face floated before her eyes, but she pushed the image away.

"Sure, Mr. Baku," she said, as nonchalantly as possible.

"I heard your father was a doctor, so having dinner in a dirty place like this probably doesn't agree with you, but . . ."

"What are you talking about? I'd be happy to eat here."

"Tetsuzo, Ms. Kotani will be joining us for dinner."

Tetsuzo didn't seem to care.

Mr. Baku began preparing the meal, so Ms. Kotani asked if she could do anything to help.

"Not in this dirty old place," he replied.

She ignored his answer and went over to give him a hand.

"Were you going to broil this fish? If you were, I could do it."

"It's flounder. I was thinking I'd do it meuniere style."

Ms. Kotani was taken aback. It was surprising enough that he knew such a word, but that he could actually cook in that style was a total shock. Flounder meuniere was a special French dish. She noticed that he had set aside a head of cabbage, mushrooms, and some other ingredients.

"What are you going to do with that meat?"

"I was gonna make what's called 'stroganoff,'" he said, as he rubbed garlic into the beef. "The name makes it sound complicated, but it's just Russian-style cooked beef with ketchup."

Ms. Kotani was even more shocked than before. She had never even heard of such a dish. Far from being able to help, she wanted to beg him to teach her.

"Wherever did you learn to cook like this?"

"Oh, it's no big deal. Any idiot could learn if they've been on as many ships as I have."

"You've been on a lot of ships?"

"That's right. I've been on Japanese ships and foreign ships and . . ." He stared off into the distance as if dreaming of some faraway land.

After a while, the food was prepared, and a gorgeous, luxurious feast was laid before her: flounder meuniere, mushroom stroganoff, and borsch soup with prawn salad. It was as if they were eating at a fancy restaurant.

"Tetsuzo, do you always eat like this?" she asked, her eyes open wide in disbelief.

"We can't very well eat like this every night," Mr. Baku explained, "but he usually gets a healthy meal."

That explained why Tetsuzo had such good manners when he ate his school lunch. Unlike other students, he rarely wolfed down his meal or left anything on his plate. Students nowadays had horrible table manners, so Ms. Kotani had been especially impressed with Tetsuzo. She watched how skillfully he handled his knife and fork.

"Tetsuzo, you wouldn't have any trouble at all if you went abroad," she said.

Mr. Baku told Ms. Kotani to help herself, so she started eating.

"Wow! This is incredibly delicious!" she exclaimed, and she obviously wasn't just being polite.

"How about something to drink?" Mr. Baku asked, offering her some beer.

"Okay," she said, accepting graciously.

"Beer is nothing for young people these days, is it?"

"I once drank two big mugs," she bragged, sounding like a juvenile delinquent.

"Wow, you can handle your liquor," said Mr. Baku, happily. "So why don't we have a drinking contest? I'm so happy to have a beautiful young woman pouring drinks for me, that I'm bound to go under first."

"You're not just a good cook; you're good at flattery, too."

Mr. Baku laughed. He really seemed to be enjoying himself.

Ms. Kotani thought he had a very nice face. Each of his wrinkles looked like a beautiful picture, and his eyes were gentle and kind. This was what Zenzai Doji would look like if he were older.

"You were handsome when you were younger, weren't you?"

"Paying me back for my compliment, huh?" said Mr. Baku, laughing.

"No, it's just that I can see where Tetsuzo gets his good looks from."

"Is that right?" said Mr. Baku, smiling even more radiantly than before.

As soon as dinner was over, Tetsuzo ran off to work on his fly drawings.

"He's been like this ever since you gave him that book, but I'm happy about it. It used to be that he couldn't do anything but play with his flies or pick fleas off Lucky, but now he's drawing pictures and writing. You've made a huge difference."

Tetsuzo's drawings covered the walls.

"Tetsuzo, how many pictures do you think you've done?" asked Ms. Kotani.

In answer, he raised his head and looked around at the pictures on the walls.

"Would you mind telling me how old you are?" asked Mr.

Baku abruptly.

"I'm twenty-two, but why do you ask?"

"Twenty-two? Is that right? Twenty-two . . ." He again stared off into the distance. "When I was twenty-two, I was in Korea."

"Really? You were in Korea when you were young?"

In lieu of an answer, he stared off into space for a while.

"Have you ever betrayed a friend?" he muttered, half to himself.

"Over something trivial, perhaps, but I don't remember now."

"Is that right?"

The joy had vanished from his face.

"When I was young, I was a student at Waseda University."

Ms. Kotani was bowled over again. Waseda was one of the most prestigious universities in Japan.

"And I had a good friend, you know, a really great guy. He was a Korean named Ryusei Kim. In all my life, I've never met such a great man."

He blinked his eyes as if trying to recall the distant past.

"At the time, Korea was a Japanese colony,[2] and Kim decided to study the history of his unfortunate country. He joined a history group, so that he could study about Korea with some others. He didn't throw a bomb or kill anybody or anything, but because he was studying about his country, he was thrown in jail. Have you ever heard of anything so stupid?"

Mr. Baku's face was contorted with pain.

"So Kim was thrown in jail. And because I was his friend, I

was drawn into it, too."

Ms. Kotani felt sick at heart.

"Ms. Kotani, do you have any idea what torture's like? Human beings will do almost anything. If they're told to act like the devil, that's exactly what they'll do. I was tortured and told to cough up the names of the members of Kim's group. They hung me from the ceiling and hit me with a bamboo cane. I had thought such things only happened in samurai times, but I sure was wrong about that. I was young at the time, so I talked back and was beaten half to death. But a person can be defiant for only so long. After having an ice pick pushed up under your fingernails, and boiling water thrown on you, your body and soul turns into a quivering mess."

Ms. Kotani's body began to shiver, and she struggled to sit still.

"I'm Japanese, so that was the worst of it for me, but interrogations of Koreans were much more violent, so it made me sick to think of what was happening to Kim. I had held firm, but Kim's mother came to me and begged me to confess. She said that if Kim had to endure any more torture, he'd probably die, but that he wouldn't talk no matter what they did to him. She pleaded with me to give them what they wanted. She was crying, and said that after one or two years in jail, I'd be free again. What she said was true, and I didn't think it would do any good to die. Considering the torture I had already received, that was a real possibility for Kim. And so, I confessed."

"Did that save him?" asked Ms. Kotani, with her heart in her mouth.

"Not in the least!" said Mr. Baku, and swallowing hard, he continued. "Kim returned home in silence with a face like a bumpy potato streaked with red paint. We'd never be able to talk together again. We'd never be able to drink together. We'd never be able to play the cello together. He returned in silence with a body that made all those things impossible. Kim's mother was a great lady. From that time on, she never shed another tear. 'I don't blame you,' she said, forgiving me, 'but since Ryusei's life is over, I want you to live, not just for yourself, but for him, too.' I love and respect Korea and the Korean people from the bottom of my heart because it's the country that gave birth to Kim and his mother.

"At the time, Japan treated Korean people like they were trash, or even worse, but secretly I thought that the damn racist fools would soon be made to pay the price. When Kim died, I totally lost interest in my studies, and perhaps drawn by his spirit, I applied to a company called the Oriental Development Company.[3] I didn't really try to find out what they did. I applied because I knew I'd be able to work in Korea. At the time, I thought I should try to make amends for what had been done to Kim."

Ms. Kotani listened attentively and held her body rigid. It somehow seemed wrong to move.

"I ended up in a section of the company called the Land Acquisition Department, and after a short while, I found out what they were up to. It was shocking how cunning Japanese could be. The government would trick perfectly innocent Koreans out of their land and make it their own. At the time, most Korean farmers couldn't read, so the Japanese made them fill out extremely difficult forms. And then when the farmers couldn't do it, they claimed that the land wasn't owned, and on that pretense, they confiscated it. The company's business was to buy up the land from the government for next to nothing and try to peddle it off to Japanese immigrants, but towards the end, they took on the job of swindling Koreans as well. When I found out about the scam they were pulling, I was glad that I had joined their company."

Mr. Baku paused.

"Why was that?" asked Ms. Kotani.

"I thought I could help the Korean people by lessening the amount of land being stolen from them. But such thinking turned out to be overly optimistic. After about three months, I was arrested by the military police. I cursed God from the bottom of my heart. In a mere three months, simply by taking sides with the Koreans, I had learned the names of two or three people involved in the Korean liberation movement. Torture at the hands of the military is much, much worse than what you get from the police. Young women like yourself would almost certainly faint if they heard about what they do. It's not just that it's too horrible to describe, it's also too humiliating to talk about. It's not your body but your heart and mind that get mangled first."

Mr. Baku closed his eyes tightly as if recalling the pain of the experience, and Ms. Kotani felt a scream welling up in her heart.

"Human beings are truly weak creatures. After only three days, I would have said anything. Two days after my confession, the military police showed me the results of my having talked. There were, oh, I don't know, maybe twelve or thirteen homes. They were burned completely to the ground so that there wasn't a trace left. Charred bodies were lying all over the place. There were small corpses, too, so obviously they didn't show any mercy for the women or children. Everyone was killed. A little while ago, I said that people could even become the devil. Well, I was talking about myself. Do you know what I thought when I saw all those corpses lying on the ground? I didn't feel regret about the horrible thing that I had done. No, before anything else, I felt overwhelming joy that my own life had been spared. How can I possibly apologize to Kim? And how can I possibly apologize to his mother?"

Mr. Baku struggled to hold back the tears.

"Once a person turns bad, it's a slippery slope and they just get worse. I knew if I remained silent, no one would ever know what happened. After that, I gave myself over to the standard ways of forgetting the past: drinking and women. I boarded one ship after another and became a drifter."

"Don't blame yourself like that," Ms. Kotani whispered to herself. "Anyone else in your position would have done the same thing."

"But even I, who had sunk to such depths, was blessed with happiness. I married late, and we had a baby girl. I got a boat, which wasn't big but which was an honest-to-goodness boat, and I went into business transporting rock from Shodo Island to Kobe. We weren't rich, but we didn't have any inconveniences either. My daughter grew up and got married, and as luck would have it, her husband was willing to go into business with me. I helped my employees set out on their own, and we kept the business in the family. During those days, my wife stayed at home to take care of the baby, who was just born, and my daughter and her husband worked on the boat with me. Well, on the day it happened, my wife had to go to Kobe, so she left the baby with a neighbor, and the four of us set off together. The weather was fine up until the Ie Islands, but right about where Awaji Island comes into view, it suddenly turned bad. Sailors are by nature very nervous about the weather, and we rarely missed the mark, but for some reason or other, it was really bad that day. The boat sunk into the ocean like a rock. We were loaded with stone, so that's how it felt. It was over in a second. We didn't even have time to think about what to do. My daughter's husband could swim, but he must have hit his head against something when the boat went down."

Ms. Kotani glanced over at Tetsuzo. He was innocently drawing his pictures.

"I suppose you could say that the sins of the past had returned to haunt me, but that's not how I saw it. Such an interpretation would have been another offense to Kim, his mother, and all the Korean people. If you saw everything in terms of grudges, then I'd be the source of grudges with the Korean people, and inside I'd be nothing but a bunch of holes. His mother told me that since she forgave me for what I did, she wanted me to live not only for myself but for her son as well. If I hadn't persevered and gone on living, it would've been my third betrayal of Ryusei Kim. So I clenched my teeth and went on."

Ms. Kotani felt warm tears welling up inside her.

"I'm sorry for making you cry. I said we'd have a drinking contest, and then I end up talking about all this stuff. I'm sorry."

"Not at all," said Ms. Kotani. "Now I know why you have such a beautiful face. And why you have such kind eyes."

Mr. Baku pulled a large, beautifully wrapped package out of the closet. He opened it and pulled out a cello.

"This is Ryusei Kim's," said Mr. Baku, caressing the cello fondly. "He and I used to love to play."

"Do you still play?"

"No, I don't. But it won't be long before we can play together again. Until then, I'll just keep his cello like this."

Ms. Kotani nodded quietly.

11. The Jellyfish Kid

In October, an unusual student by the name of Minako Ito joined Ms. Kotani's class. Minako loved to run, but if "running" meant to go faster than usual, then it wasn't exactly running. Minako ran whenever she was happy or feeling good, and the running usually made her laugh.

As she ran, she would look up into the air and start flapping her arms and legs. If a person were to copy how a jellyfish swims, it would be a close imitation of Minako's running. That was why she didn't pick up any speed, and why she sometimes tripped and fell. When Minako was running around the classroom, the students could tell that she was in a good mood.

In the morning, Minako's grandmother would bring Minako to school and show her to her seat, and for a short time, Minako would sit at her desk like other students. But she couldn't sit still for more than a few minutes, and before long, she would start wandering around the room. Then, she would start playing with her classmates' belongings. Sometimes, she would put one of their erasers in her mouth and pretend she was eating it. When the student asked for it back, Minako would smile and return it when she was in a good mood, but if she were in a bad mood, she would throw it across the room. And then she would start wandering around again. At other times, she just skirted around the room like a jellyfish. Minako always had to be doing something and that usually meant causing trouble for someone else.

Ms. Kotani would come into class. The children would take their seats, and one seat would be empty. It was Minako's seat, of course, but the problem was that Minako didn't know it.

"Minako, here is your seat," Ms. Kotani would say, taking her by the hand. Minako would sit down and the class would begin, but before long, she would come to the front of the room, take Ms. Kotani's hand, and smile. Sometimes, she would start swinging, which made her giggle noisily.

Ms. Kotani would give the students something to do, and bring Minako back to her seat. Then she would give her some drawing paper and show her how to draw a circle or a triangle with a crayon. She would also show her how to color. When Minako finally started to play with the crayons, Ms. Kotani would dash to the front of the room and begin to teach. The process was repeated several times each period. Ms. Kotani had to be quick and agile like a ninja, and it was extremely strenuous labor.

There were many other problems, too. Such as the times when Minako yelled, "Pee-pee!" Minako would chatter on about various things and sometimes she would sing, but Ms. Kotani and the students could never understand her. She sounded like a small child jumbling up the words to a song she didn't know. But one word of hers everyone understood, and that word always spelt trouble. When Ms. Kotani heard "pee-pee," she would rush Minako to the bathroom as quickly as she could, but they rarely made it in time. Usually, Minako wet her pants on the way, but sometimes, she wet them before the word of warning was halfway out of her mouth.

"She did it again!" the students would yell in unison.

The students were amused, but it was a major chore for Ms. Kotani. Cleaning up the mess usually took five or six minutes, and during that time, the class had to be left unattended, which was extremely aggravating.

Every morning, Minako's grandmother handed Ms. Kotani three clean pairs of underwear. Though they rarely used all of them, they needed at least that many to feel safe.

"I truly am sorry," Minako's grandmother would say, bowing so many times that she began to look pathetic.

"It's no trouble at all," Ms. Kotani would answer, smiling affably. Her smile infected some of her students, and sometimes they would bow and smile alongside her.

But Ms. Kotani was only human. When Minako wet herself right in the middle of saying "pee-pee" just before lunch or at other busy times, she had to fight back a violent urge to yell at her.

"Damn pissing jellyfish!" she would mutter to herself.

But she never said such things to Minako and always managed to keep up a smile. When Ms. Kotani agreed to have Minako join her class, she made two promises to herself: she swore to look after her to the end, and she swore that no matter what, she would never complain. She also swore not to cry, but she knew that she was too much of a crybaby to keep such a promise, so she gave that up.

Long ago, when people prayed for something, they would swear to put up with all hardships until the prayer was answered, and as evidence of their resolve, they would make some kind of sacrifice, such as giving up meat or tea. Ms. Kotani was young, so she didn't follow such an old-fashioned tradition, but when it came to fulfilling what she swore to, she was a lot like the people of old.

Ms. Kotani's decision to take on Minako came shortly after hearing Mr. Baku's disturbing story. She wanted the beauty of Zenzai Doji and the kindness of Mr. Baku to live in her, and she even felt that that could be her goal in life. In exaggerated terms, she took on Minako to change how she had been living, and since that was her purpose, she couldn't very well make a fuss over every little thing. If she couldn't keep up a smile over something like "pee-pee," then her future did not bode well.

Lunchtime was especially difficult because Minako couldn't use a spoon very well. She would make an effort at first, but when it turned out to be too difficult, she would switch to grabbing the food with her hands, and if the food was hot, it became quite an affair. She would throw the food away after grabbing it, and if she got soup or gravy on her hands, she would just shake it off. The students sitting next to her couldn't stand it: some would knock over their milks trying to run away, and others would scream and yell. The entire classroom would soon be thrown into pandemonium.

On top of all this, Minako couldn't distinguish between what was hers and someone else's and would sometimes grab the food of the student sitting next to her.

"Junichi, please forgive her," Ms. Kotani would say, as she replaced the food that Minako had taken.

Junichi would look disgusted, which was natural enough. You needed a bit of courage to eat something that someone had stuck their hand in. Sometimes, Ms. Kotani hurriedly traded her own food tray with the student just to avoid a scene.

The biggest problem of all, however, was when Minako left the classroom and wandered off. If Ms. Kotani took her eyes off her for even a second, she would fly off like the wind. Minako preferred to be outside, and laughing happily, she would float off like a swaying jellyfish.

In a panic, Ms. Kotani would rush off to look for her. A child like Minako was not afraid of bicycles or manholes, so danger was everywhere. After searching all over for her, a pale and terrified Ms. Kotani would find her playing with the school's goat or wading in the pond up to her waist and chasing after the goldfish. Such times were extremely trying, but Minako seemed truly happy. When Ms. Kotani saw her smiling face, she just couldn't stay angry at her.

A week had passed, and Ms. Kotani still hadn't explained to her students about Minako or about her reasons for having her join the class. Minako was home with a cold, so it was the perfect opportunity to bring up the subject.

After the class finished discussing the different problems that Minako had been causing them, a girl named Haruko blurted out, "Minako's a real idiot, isn't she, Ms. Kotani?"

"She's the king of idiots," added Katsuichi, the class clown. Everyone laughed.

"What do you mean by 'idiot'?" asked Ms. Kotani.

"A kid who's not very smart."

"A kid who can't study."

"Well, your mothers say the same thing about you."

"Oops," the students seemed to be thinking.

"Long ago, idiot children used to be killed or thrown away," said Ms. Kotani. She conveyed the horrible information as if she were reading from a picture book.

"No way!" the students yelled.

"It's true. In Greece, there's still a mountain called Mt. Taygetos, where children like Minako used to be killed. In Japan, as you know, old people who were a burden used to be left in the mountains to die. For children, they used to put them in reed boats and wash them down the river."

Some of the girls hugged each other in fear as they listened to their teacher's explanation.

"But why'd they have to go and kill 'em?" one of them cried.

"Probably 'cause they caused trouble for everyone," answered a boy named Takeshi.

"Minako causes a lot of trouble, too, doesn't she?" said Ms. Kotani.

A hush came over the students as they wondered what their teacher would say next.

"But we cause a lot of trouble for our mothers," protested Takeshi, as if trying to erase the damage of his previous comment.

"Is Minako comin' in tomorrow, Ms. Kotani?" asked Katsuichi, who had usually avoided using Minako's name.

"I have no idea," said Ms. Kotani, tormenting them.

"Oh, she's coming in, isn't she?" called out a student unable to bear it.

"She is, isn't she?" called out another.

"Do you want her to?"

"Yeh, we do!" called out the students in unison.

"Even if she causes trouble?"

"Yeh! It's okay!" they yelled, and Takeshi's voice was the loudest of all.

They were no doubt imagining how horrible it would be if Minako were taken away to Mt. Taygetos.

Ms. Kotani's determination to keep Minako in the class, however, was soon put to the test. She was reading student compositions in the teachers' room when the Assistant Principal came over to her desk.

"You're wanted in the principal's office," he said, obviously in a bad mood.

When they entered the principal's office together, over a dozen parents were waiting for her.

"Some parents want to talk to you," said the Principal, looking annoyed.

"What is it?"

"It's about that Minako Ito," he answered, wiping the sweat from his forehead. "I've already explained the general situation, but they would like to hear from you." His sweating didn't seem entirely due to the heat.

"First, we'd like to hear your views for getting involved in Miss Ito's education," said Junichi's mother. She was the manager of the steelworks and spoke in stilted Japanese.

"I don't have any special views at all. My attitude towards her is the same as it is towards the other children."

"Well then, tell me this. I hear that you made a special request to the Principal to get her into your class. We just heard that even though she'll be enrolling in a school for the handicapped in November, she applied to our school to take charge of her during the one-month wait. Now what's this? The school turned her down once, but then you came along and begged to have her in your class. That sounds a bit unusual if you don't have any special reason for doing so, don't you think?"

"I did fully explain about your eagerness," said the Principal in a vacillating tone. The Assistant Principal made a sour face. He had been opposed to the idea from the very beginning.

Ms. Kotani debated with herself about how to respond. To

accurately convey her views, an hour or two's discussion would be woefully inadequate, and even if she could make herself understood, they still might not agree with her. She decided to keep it simple.

"I felt that if Minako became part of the class, everyone would benefit."

"You must be joking!" one of the parents in the back screamed hysterically. "Do you even realize what you're saying? My son says that he can't get a single thing done all day!"

Ms. Kotani thought what the woman said was horrible, but she bit her tongue.

"You can do whatever you want during your free time, but when your little hobbies start causing problems for others, then it's a completely different story. Don't you agree, everybody?"

Ms. Kotani was young, and she began to get frustrated.

"I'm not doing this for my own amusement! I'm doing the best that I can!"

"We're not denying your passion," another parent said calmly. "But just as Miss Ito's mother is looking out for her daughter, we're looking out for our children, too. We've come here today to ask for your help because we're worried that as the way things stand, our children's education might suffer."

"I think you've been playing favorites," put in another parent.

Ms. Kotani's face hardened. She had been patient, but that was the last straw.

"When you came to our homes for the teacher visits, you

refused to even have a cup of tea. And no matter how many times we offered, you just kept saying it was the school rule. But then you go off to another student's house, and don't just have tea, but an entire meal! Isn't that right?"

Ms. Kotani wanted to bury her head in the sand.

"Some mothers have been really resentful about that."

It was beginning to seem like a public hanging, and the Assistant Principal couldn't stand it any longer.

"How about it, Ms. Kotani?" he asked. "Would you be willing to reconsider your position on this issue?"

Ms. Kotani immediately turned and faced him. "I am *not* giving up Minako!"

"But why on earth are you so stuck on her?" said Junichi's mother. "Whom are you doing this for?"

"I'm doing it for myself," said Ms. Kotani frankly. The mothers broke into a commotion.

"I'm shocked. Don't schoolteachers work for the benefit of the students?"

"I work for myself. I don't know about other teachers."

"Well, this simply won't do," said several parents in disgust.

"Mr. Baku, please help me!" pleaded Ms. Kotani in silence. "I've spoken honestly. I took your error upon myself, but that was all I could say. Was I wrong? Please tell me!" She closed her eyes tightly, and implored him to guide her.

Not surprisingly, Ms. Kotani wasn't up for visiting anyone that day, and in her heart, she beseeched Tetsuzo to forgive her laziness.

12. Cloudy, Later Sunny

The next day, Ms. Kotani had to struggle to drag herself into school. When she felt that way during the first semester, she never hesitated to take some time off, but that wasn't possible this time, so she reluctantly hauled herself in.

Minako was waiting at the front gate with her parents and grandmother, so Ms. Kotani wondered what was going on.

"Minako, what's wrong?" she asked. "Is your cold all better? There's no need to push yourself."

As soon as Minako saw Ms. Kotani, she smiled happily. Ms. Kotani helped Minako blow her nose and rejoiced at having decided to come to work. Looking at Minako's smiling face, she felt as if a load had been lifted from her shoulders.

"Ms. Kotani," said Minako's mother, pressing a handkerchief to her eyes.

"What wrong?" asked Ms. Kotani, becoming alarmed.

"Ms. Kotani . . . yesterday . . . just for Minako . . ." Her words faded into sobs.

"The Assistant Principal paid us a visit last night," said Minako's father, picking up for his wife. "And he gave us all the details of yesterday's big scene. He said that we've caused you enough trouble and that we should offer to withdraw Minako from the school."

"What a thing to say!" said Ms. Kotani. She was furious at the Assistant Principal for being so cowardly and mean as to take advantage of their weak position.

"Even yesterday," said Minako's mother, starting to cry again, "Minako grabbed her bag . . . and pulled her grandmother's hand to go . . ."

"I'll take care of Minako to the end. Don't you worry."

"But the Assistant Principal said that . . ."

"I'll talk to him myself," said Ms. Kotani, trying to sound pleasant. "Okay, Minako, let's go."

Ms. Kotani's class was relieved when Minako showed up for class that day, and more students than usual played with her during recess. She caused as much trouble as before, but Ms. Kotani continued to take care of her with a smile.

The student who had suffered the most since Minako joined the class was Junichi, a quiet boy who sat next to her. Minako was always tearing up Junichi's notebooks, and when she started to tear up one of his textbooks, too, he nearly started to sob.

Early on, Junichi had had a hard time dealing with her. When she grabbed his food, he made a fuss, and when she stole his pencil, he jumped up and grabbed it away from her. But after a while, his attitude towards Minako started to change, and a similar change could be seen in the entire class.

Now, when Minako started to tear his notebook, he remained calm.

"Gimme back my notebook, Minako," he would say quietly.

Sometimes she tore it anyway, and sometimes she returned it unscathed, but she usually gave him a smile. And when he got his notebook back, Junichi would smile, too. From the outside, it looked like they were playing some kind of private game. Sometimes Junichi would hand her an old notebook that he no longer needed.

"Here, tear this," he would say.

Whenever Minako actually did tear one of his notebooks, Junichi would sigh resignedly and say, "Oh, Minako, you really shouldn't tear people's notebooks." If he could say that without yelling, Minako usually smiled, and then he would smile in return. They truly seemed to be enjoying each other.

During lunchtime, Junichi put his tray where Minako couldn't reach it, but when her plate became empty, he would ask her if she wanted more. If her eyes started roaming around the room, he gave her some of his. And then if she smiled, everyone could relax because they knew she wouldn't grab anyone else's.

Junichi was quick to raise his hand when they held their next class meeting on Minako.

"Is Minako a lot of trouble for you, Ms. Kotani?" he asked.

"Yes, she is," answered Ms. Kotani honestly.

"But you're really into her, aren't you? I mean, you like her, right?"

"Yes, I do," she answered, smiling. Junichi's carefree way of talking always amused her.

"She's a lot of trouble, but she's cute. That's why you don't know what to do, right? And that's why you're talking it out with us."

"That's right." Junichi was so cute when he talked this way.

"Well, I thought of a good idea."

"What is it, Junichi?"

"Why don't we have Minako duty?"

"'Minako duty'?"

"Yeh, the person on cleaning duty does the cleaning, right? And the person on day duty opens the windows and takes the roll, right? Well, the person on Minako duty would take care of Minako. They'd play with her and study with her and stay next to her all the time."

"That's a good idea. But she's not easy to take care of, you know. If you watched me during the day, you'd see what I mean."

"Ms. Kotani," said Junichi, raising his hand again. "Do you wanna hear how I came up with my idea? Minako tore my notebook, but I didn't get mad. She tore my book, but I didn't get mad. She took my pencil case and my eraser, but I didn't get mad, and we played train instead. I didn't get mad at her, and that's why I started to like her. And if you start to like her, it doesn't bother you when she causes trouble. She just seems cute."

Ms. Kotani was struck with admiration. Junichi had asked if Minako was a lot of trouble, and she had given an honest answer, but after hearing his explanation, she could see that he had been testing her. He was telling her that she shouldn't just see Minako as being a nuisance. And on top of that, he wanted to create an opportunity for everyone in the class to learn the same thing.

"Junichi, you really are smart," she said, speaking from the heart.

The vote for Minako duty was unanimous, and the class agreed to start the next day. Each day, a pair of one boy and one girl would take care of Minako, the order to be decided by lottery. When they drew their lots, students that ended up with early turns rejoiced, and those that ended up with late turns grieved.

When school let out that day, Ms. Kotani paid a visit to Katsuichi's house, which doubled as a meat shop. As soon as she walked in the door, Katsuichi's father jumped up.

"Ms. Kotani," he said excitedly, "could you come upstairs for a minute?"

When she reached the second floor, she was shocked: there were as many parents here as had come to the principal's office the day before. The faces, though, were different, most of these parents being from the shopping district and other downtown areas.

"Ms. Kotani, we heard about what happened yesterday, and we want you to know that we're on your side. And we're not the only ones."

Ms. Kotani could see that the incident had begun to turn into a complicated mess.

"It's really pretty disgusting! Giving you a hard time for pouring out your heart and soul to help a kid that's a little less fortunate! What on earth could those people be thinking? Even when you're finished with classes, you go around visiting kids' homes like this. Even if it's only five minutes or so, that's a big help for kids that have fallen behind. I don't think there's many other teachers like that."

"But they do have a point," cut in Ms. Kotani, in distress. "It's true that I'm inexperienced, and since I took on Minako, we've been starting to fall behind. I can understand why they're worried."

"I hope you don't mean that," said Katsuichi's father, who was still young. "Because if you do, then I have to say, you're gravely mistaken. That's just looking at things in terms of short-term gain. I'm no expert on education, but I can't agree with the attitude of just looking out for number one. Sure, I sound overly optimistic. If you don't have the cutthroat attitude, you're not gonna make it in the real world. But it's precisely because I know that's how it is, that I'm saying what I'm saying. And that's why we need the schools to teach about kindness and consideration. I know I sound awfully old-fashioned, but those of us in business need such ideas if our customers are gonna trust us. It's those human connections that make life worth living. Am I wrong?"

Ms. Kotani didn't think he was.

"If we don't say anything, the school's gonna think that none of the parents support you. What we have to say is fair enough, so we're thinking of heading down to see the Principal right now and giving him a piece of our mind."

Ms. Kotani told them that she appreciated their concern, but that she preferred they not do anything. She also told them about that day's class discussion.

"So you see, starting tomorrow, we're getting behind Minako and making a new start. The children and I are really excited about it. And I'd really appreciate it if you could just quietly watch over the situation from the outside."

"We understand," said Katsuichi's father, like a man. "How about it, everyone? Should we leave it to Ms. Kotani?"

No one was opposed.

"Ms. Kotani, we're on your side," said one of the mothers to encourage her. "If there's any problem, please let us know."

"And don't get so carried away about your students that you neglect your husband," said the owner of a fish shop.

"That's right. Nothing would upset us more than if you ended up getting divorced."

"But if you do, let me know," joked Katsuichi's father, "because I'll dump my current wife and marry you. If you'll have me, of course."

Everyone burst out laughing.

They were such good-natured people. Yesterday, she was in tears, and today she was laughing. First, it's cloudy, and then it's sunny. She felt completely reinvigorated.

Ms. Kotani said goodbye and headed over to Tetsuzo's house.

"Sorry about yesterday, Tetsuzo. I was being lazy."

"Ah."

Tetsuzo's standard reply had recently changed from "uh" to "ah." Ms. Kotani felt that the "ah" had more feeling behind it.

"So, Professor, how were the results of your experiment?" she asked in a playful tone of voice. She was in a great mood.

Tetsuzo brought over the close-lined notebook and showed it to her.

"It'll be one week tomorrow," she said, leafing through the notebook, "but the results are pretty clear already, aren't they?"

For the experiment, they used five bottles and the following four kinds of flies: houseflies, blowflies, green bottle flies, and flesh flies. Ten of each species were put separately into four of the bottles, and five of each were mixed together in the fifth.

Tetsuzo was researching their eating habits, and three times a day, he recorded which flies swarmed to which foods. Strictly speaking, swarming around a certain food didn't necessarily mean the fly was feeding, but since Tetsuzo was only a first-grader, Ms. Kotani didn't think they needed to be so exact.

They used flies that were relatively numerous and closely related to the everyday lives of human beings. Tetsuzo hadn't been raising houseflies, but without such an important fly, his research would have been meaningless, so Ms. Kotani convinced him to include them.

Flies feed on innumerable things, so deciding on what foods to use and how to classify them was a problem. Ms. Kotani considered dividing them into animal foods and plant foods, and then considered categorizing them as nutritionists do into fats, proteins, and sugars, but she wouldn't have been able to explain such difficult concepts to Tetsuzo. Instead, she went with Tetsuzo to the garbage dump and had him point to anything that flies feed on. The things he pointed to included fish, shellfish, decaying animal flesh, animal skins, fruit, rotten vegetables, soybean paste, alcohol, sweets, tree sap, and flowers. After that, she consulted with him (though that only meant that Tetsuzo answered "ah") and narrowed it down to six items: leftover fish parts, beef, lard, fruit, rotten vegetables, and candy.

Tetsuzo already knew what different flies liked to eat, and the experiment probably wasn't very interesting for him, but he willingly played along. He faithfully took records three times a day: before going to school, after he returned home, and once in the evening. And he never missed a day.

"Tetsuzo, from this, it's very clear that the blow flies, green bottle flies, and flesh flies like fish and meat."

"Ah."

"Houseflies seem to prefer fruit and candy, but from your records, it's clear that they'll eat almost anything. You also mentioned that they like to eat people's poop, so I guess houseflies are the biggest gluttons of all. Right?"

"Ah."

"None of the flies like oily things. They almost never swarmed to the lard."

"Ah."

"Oh, and here's something interesting. For the candy, the number of flies stayed about the same everyday, but for the fruit, meat, and fish, which began to rot, the number changed from day to day. Look at this. For the fish, the number of flies was largest on the third day, and for the fruit, on the fifth day."

Ms. Kotani started to get excited.

"Tetsuzo, this is a great discovery. Flies won't swarm to fish if it's too fresh or too old. So you can tell whether the fish is fresh or not, just by the number of flies. That means if you see any flies around the fish at the market, you shouldn't buy it, right?"

It was funny that Ms. Kotani was sounding like a housewife as she discussed flies and garbage. Tetsuzo didn't seem to think the discovery was such a big deal.

13. Minako Duty

The first two students on Minako duty were Yuji and Terue, and that morning, Minako's seat was changed so that she sat between them. When Junichi waved goodbye, Minako smiled and waved in return, but when the first period class began, she immediately walked back to her old seat.

"Minako, you can't come over here anymore," said Junichi, taking her by the hand and returning her to her new seat. Then he turned to Yuji and said, "You're supposed to be takin' care of her."

Ms. Kotani looked on quietly and smiled. When she agreed to the plan, she had resolved to stay out of it as much as possible.

About halfway through the first period, Minako gave up on visiting Junichi and tottered out the door. As if on cue, Yuji and Terue dashed out after her. Yuji didn't like to study and had been waiting for just such an opportunity. Ms. Kotani chuckled to herself.

"Look, Minako, I'm a butterfly," said Yuji, flapping his arms. Released from the classroom, he was now in high spirits. Minako giggled loudly and became a butterfly, too.

The three butterflies headed out to the playground, and Butterfly Minako started to run. The other two butterflies had so much trouble keeping up with her that sweat was soon dripping from their noses.

A group of sixth-graders who were having gym class looked

over at them suspiciously.

"What are those guys up to?" one of them asked.

After running around the playground to their heart's content, the three decided to play on the sliding board. Minako loved to climb up to high places, but her arms and legs weren't very strong. Ms. Kotani had warned the students many times that if Minako climbed up somewhere, they should go with her and make sure she held on to something. So when Minako climbed the sliding board, Yuji and Terue climbed up after her.

Sliding boards were not so popular anymore. First-graders played on them for the first few weeks or so, but after that, they were just left to rust and get dirty.

Minako slid down the rusty old sliding board in a flash, and Yuji and Terue hurriedly slid down behind her.

"Our butts are all red," moaned Terue pathetically.

"Yeh, really," said Yuji.

Minako smiled and raced up again. The other two scurried up after her. Minako slid down. The other two slid down after her.

"Minako, our butts are turning red," said Terue, trying to persuade Minako to stop. "Forget about the sliding board. Let's play on the chin-up bar, okay? You're a good little girl, aren't you? Well, let's go over there."

She patted Minako on the head in a last-ditch attempt to trick her.

"Why do you wanna keep doing the same thing over and over again?" complained Yuji. He was at his wits' end, too.

Minako yanked her hand away from Terue's and raced up the sliding board yet again.

"Our pants are gonna rip," whimpered Terue, sounding like she was going to cry.

At the end of the second period, Yuji dragged a crying Terue and a smiling Minako back to the classroom. When the other students saw their behinds, they nearly fell down laughing. The seats of their pants were full of gaping holes, and their underwear was filthy.

The first day of Minako duty turned out to be extremely difficult, and at the end of the day, Yuji and Terue received a round of applause. When Minako's grandmother thanked them for their hard work, they were all smiles.

Ms. Kotani knew that they would sleep soundly that night.

Most students were well aware of the trials and tribulations of Minako duty before their turn came around. Two or three days ahead of time, they would run to someone who had already been on duty and question them about Minako. Junichi was considered the Minako expert, and he politely answered all his classmates' questions.

With the start of Minako duty, Ms. Kotani initiated a class newsletter, which informed parents about Minako duty and other events of the day. In the first newsletter, she printed out in large letters what Junichi had said the day before:

Minako tore my notebook

But I didn't get mad
She tore my book
But I didn't get mad
She took my pencil case and my eraser
But I didn't get mad
And we played train instead
I didn't get mad at her
And that's why I started to like her
And if you start to like her
It doesn't bother you when she causes trouble
She just seems cute

On the fifth day of Minako duty, there was a minor incident.

Kiyoshi and Michiko were on duty, and during the second period, they followed Minako out into the playground. They played together for a while, but then Minako started yelling "pee-pee." They hurried to get her to the bathroom, but Minako wet her pants just as they started to run.

"Now you did it," said Kiyoshi, remaining calm.

"Go get some fresh underwear from Ms. Kotani," said the strong-minded Michiko, determined to take care of the problem herself.

When Kiyoshi reported the situation, Ms. Kotani rushed to the scene.

"Oh, look at that," said Ms. Kotani, beginning to take off Minako's wet underwear.

"Ms. Kotani," said Michiko in a sharp tone of voice, "we're the ones on Minako duty."

"Oh, I'm sorry," Ms. Kotani apologized instinctively. "Could you do it, then? I'll go back to class."

"Okay, go then," said Michiko, still annoyed.

The incident occurred about a minute later.

Perhaps because she felt good without underwear, Minako tried to climb into the nearby pond, which was overgrown with algae. As soon as she got one foot in, she slipped and fell head first into the pond. Michiko waded in after her and held out her hand, but when Minako reached up and grabbed it, Michiko came tumbling down, too.

After that, the two girls were like a couple of drowned rats, and Kiyoshi started screaming and yelling. Mr. Sayama, who was having a gym class, dashed over and pulled the struggling girls out. He had slipped in the pond once, too, so there was no question about how slippery it was.

Ms. Kotani received a severe dressing down, including an especially bad scolding from the Assistant Principal. She apologized as earnestly as she could and didn't make any excuses. She didn't want to risk saying anything in explanation that might lead to Minako duty being cancelled.

Even before Minako duty started, Ms. Kotani had fully anticipated these sorts of problems. She had checked out every nook and cranny of the school grounds, and had tried to imagine what kinds of accidents might occur at each location. She had warned the class not to take Minako to places that were especially dangerous, such as the roof or the furnace, and she had emphasized that if Minako ever tried to go to one of those places, they should stop her—even if they had to use force. Ms. Kotani didn't just explain all this. She actually walked the students around the school grounds and pointed out all the dangers directly.

Even with all the precautions, Ms. Kotani feared that there might be some minor accident. But she also felt that if you always worried about accidents, you'd never get anything done. Some teachers were not afraid to declare publicly that babysitting students and protecting them from harm was enough, but Ms. Kotani had little respect for such teachers.

Be that as it may, she left the principal's office feeling that she had received quite a bawling out, and when Mr. Orihashi asked her what was wrong, tears tumbled down her cheeks. Mr. Adachi gave her an encouraging slap on the back.

Ms. Kotani tried not to let it get to her. Tetsuzo was scheduled for Minako duty the next day, and she wondered how he would do. He was paired up with a shy, unobtrusive girl named Yayoi. If he had been paired up with a strong-willed girl like Michiko, she wouldn't have worried, but Tetsuzo and Yayoi made her nervous. She prayed that he could do a good job.

The next day, Tetsuzo appeared at school looking the same as always, while Yayoi looked extremely nervous.

During the first period, Minako took out the counting sticks and marbles, and played relatively quietly by herself. Tetsuzo seemed completely unconcerned, but this made Ms. Kotani nervous. He seemed totally apathetic about everything around him.

During the second period, Minako started to show signs of wanting to go outside, but as soon as she started to get restless, Tetsuzo got up and walked out of the room first. Minako scurried after him, and Yayoi hurriedly took up the rear.

Ms. Kotani glanced out the window to see what was going on. Tetsuzo was marching off somewhere, and Minako and Yayoi trailed behind him. This was the first time that it went like this. Up until today, the students on Minako duty did all the chasing. Ms. Kotani was intrigued.

Tetsuzo and his companions reached the cherry tree near the school entrance, and all three of them looked up with their mouths hanging open, though Minako and Yayoi were only imitating Tetsuzo.

After a while, Tetsuzo started shaking the tree, and some objects came raining down from the leaves. He collected them and gathered them into a pile. Minako and Yayoi took a peek and noticed that they were small caterpillars, about an inch and a half long. Yayoi was repulsed, but Minako poked them with her finger and shrieked with delight.

Tetsuzo picked the caterpillars up and carried them to the sandbox. Then he dug a hole and put them in for safekeeping. After that, he leveled off a section of the sand, picked up the caterpillars, and scattered them on top as if he were sprinkling salt into a kettle. Finally, he quickly covered them over with another layer of sand.

The three peeked down at the sand with their butts sticking up in the air. After about thirty seconds, squirming caterpillars started popping up all over the place in a truly bizarre fashion. Whenever a caterpillar popped up, Minako would look at the caterpillar and laugh. Then she would peek over at Tetsuzo and laugh again. She was completely captivated. Tetsuzo repeated the process two or three times, and after that, Minako started doing it herself. The caterpillars popped up no matter who buried them, and this time, Minako laughed even louder than before. She was in a great mood.

Ms. Kotani couldn't relax just watching from the window and made several trips outside to check on them. After convincing herself that all was well, she returned to the classroom. Tetsuzo didn't seem to be playing with Minako so much as just doing what he wanted. Minako, though, was thrilled.

Ms. Kotani was impressed. Up until now, the students on Minako duty were pretty much at Minako's mercy. If Minako wanted to play on the swings, they played on the swings. If she wanted to jump on the tires, they jumped on the tires. Even if they did something else, Minako would just go the other way, so it was futile to oppose her. But with Tetsuzo, it was different. He never even tried to humor her.

During the third period, they headed out of sight, and Ms. Kotani started to get nervous. She ran outside to look for them and found them behind the west wing of the school. Minako's high-pitched squeals of delight signaled that she was still enjoying herself.

The three of them were making something, and Ms. Kotani moved closer to get a better look. They had created a couple of strange-shaped sculptures out of clay, which they had made by mixing water with some red powder left behind by a construction crew.

Tetsuzo's creation had a center section that looked like a snail shell, and he had even drawn in the swirling lines. A dozen pencil-shaped legs protruded in various directions from the base, and he had broken some twigs into toothpicks, which were sticking out from the shell. It had the intriguing quality of an abstract sculpture.

Minako had merely piled up some little balls, which looked like grapes, and stuck in numerous twigs as Tetsuzo did. In its simplicity, it conveyed an unexpected kind of strength. Yayoi was helping the other two, so she hadn't made one of her own.

"These are fantastic," said Ms. Kotani, almost ashamed to be a teacher. "If Picasso saw these, he'd cry for joy."

During the fourth period, something horrible happened.

The little group finished playing with the clay and headed across the playground towards their classroom. Mr. Yamauchi, the head teacher for the fifth grade, and Mr. Ota were supervising a soccer scrimmage between their fifth-grade classes. When Minako saw the excitement, she ran out onto the field and started chasing after the ball. The whistle blew, and Mr. Yamauchi, who was officiating, yelled for Minako to get out of the way. Even with that, Minako continued to gaily chase after the ball, so Mr. Yamauchi grabbed her by the scruff of the neck and started to drag her off the field.

That was when Tetsuzo jumped on him. Mr. Yamauchi suddenly felt a sharp pain biting into his right arm. He screamed in agony and tried to shake Tetsuzo off, but when the attempt failed, he smacked Tetsuzo across the face a couple of times. Mr. Ota came running up, and barely managed to pull Tetsuzo away, but since he had seen the whole thing, he couldn't refrain from being critical of Mr. Yamauchi.

"That was out of line," he said.

"What!" shot back Mr. Yamauchi.

That initiated a violent argument. Mr. Ota was a young new teacher like Ms. Kotani, and once he got fired up about something, he didn't back down. Perhaps because they felt self-conscious arguing in front of the students, the two teachers returned to the teachers' room, but their dispute only escalated.

Mr. Yamauchi's eyes turned red, and Mr. Ota's face turned pale. Just then, the noon recess bell rang, and the other teachers started returning from their classes.

"Resign, you impertinent thing!" screamed Mr. Yamauchi.

"Resign? You're the one that should resign!" shot back Mr. Ota. "You have a lot of nerve to go on teaching after sending students off to battle in the Pacific War!"

Nothing bothered someone from Mr. Yamauchi's generation

more than that accusation, and he instinctively grabbed Mr. Ota by the collar.

"Stop it!" screamed one of the female teachers.

"Knock it off!" yelled Mr. Adachi. "Let's hear what Mr. Ota has to say!"

The Assistant Principal started yelling at Mr. Adachi for taking sides, and Mr. Adachi yelled back at him. It had developed into a four-teacher fight.

Ms. Kotani caught wind of what was happening and dashed to the teachers' room, but when she saw what was happening, she broke down in tears.

"Get him, Adachi! Get him!"

"Do it, Ota! Do it!"

Isao, Jun, and some of the disposal plant children had suddenly appeared in the window and were cheering for their favorite teachers.

14. Don't Cry, Ms. Kotani

Ms. Kotani was sniveling like a baby.

"He's a piece of shit!" yelled Mr. Ota, still white with rage.

"Take it easy," said Mr. Adachi, a black circle forming under his left eye.

"It's nothing to cry about, Ms. Kotani," said Mr. Orihashi, with a troubled look.

"That's right, it's nothing to cry about," seconded Mr. Ota.

Left to their own devices, the teachers were unlikely to settle down and were at risk of losing control again, so Mr. Adachi took them out to a bar for a drink. Mr. Orihashi and Mr. Ota were especially close friends.

"I got in some good punches during the confusion," said Mr. Adachi, provocatively, "but this black eye looks a hell of a lot worse."

"You can't go pretending to be Botchan[4] and hit the Principal and Assistant Principal," said the woman behind the bar. "Hitting the Principal can only lead to this."

She made a gesture of cutting her own throat.

"I wish you'd try a little harder to keep your jobs. We don't have many good teachers these days, so I wish you'd be more careful."

"Yeh, I know. Just bring me a bottle of sake," answered Mr. Adachi, with a grimace. Apparently, the pain was starting to set in.

Ms. Kotani couldn't help feeling sorry for Tetsuzo. He had fulfilled his duty so well, only to have things turn out so horribly. Why couldn't Mr. Yamauchi have given Minako a little hug when he was moving her out of the way? Or at the very least, why didn't he just take her hand? If he had, Tetsuzo would never have jumped on him. Why did this have to happen right when Tetsuzo was doing such a great job and was starting to make a friend? When she imagined how Tetsuzo must have been feeling when he tried to protect Minako like that, she could barely stand it. Her heart really went out to him.

When she had taken Tetsuzo home and was explaining everything to Mr. Baku, she couldn't stop crying. Mr. Baku stared at her with his kind eyes and gently rubbed Tetsuzo's head with his large hand.

"That's my grandson for you," he had said. "Tetsuzo's a good kid. I'm sure Minako will never forget what he did for her."

The three male teachers drank at a rapid pitch. It wasn't clear whether they were drinking out of anger or out of despair, but they were certainly drinking more than usual.

"Maybe I was a bit out of line," said Mr. Ota. "Sure, he hit me first, but I shouldn't have laid a hand on an older teacher. It's just that I've put up with a lot from him up to now. When I put together a booklet of my class's writings, he made sarcastic comments, and when we had teacher visits, he told me not to be such a popularity-seeker. Reptilian humans like him are pretty rare. He actually said I should have been more considerate of teachers that might've wanted to make booklets but couldn't. What the hell does that have to do with me?"

"Hey, that's how it is at every grade level," said Mr. Orihashi, speaking sluggishly. "But instead of getting worked up about guys like him, you'd be better off trying to get other teachers to see your point of view."

"I guess I'm not the pushover that you are," said Mr. Ota, starting to take out his anger on his friend. "Before laying back and taking that approach, I just wanna beat the hell out of the bad guys."

"All right, play the brute, if you prefer. But can't you see that the real bad guys are the ones that are too slick for us even to notice?"

Mr. Adachi burst out laughing.

"You two should quit teaching and become stand-up comedians."

"Sure, go ahead and make jokes," said Mr. Orihashi, reproachfully. "Here, Ms. Kotani, have something to drink."

Mr. Orihashi poured her some sake, and Ms. Kotani drained her glass in one gulp. Mr. Orihashi and Mr. Ota exchanged glances.

"Sorry for causing you so much trouble," said Ms. Kotani.

"Oh, cheer up," said Mr. Ota, comforting her.

"Mr. Adachi, how's your eye feeling?" she asked.

"Before asking about others, maybe you should take a look at your own," said Mr. Adachi.

Ms. Kotani took out her compact. Her eyes were all swollen and red.

"You're a fine woman, but I wish you'd do something about all this whimpering. I can't stand it."

"I'm sorry," said Ms. Kotani, and she looked like she might start crying again.

"Come now, you're acting like a schoolgirl," said Mr. Adachi. "Since you've arrived, I've lost about six pounds from stress and worry."

"You have?" asked Mr. Orihashi, teasing him.

The next day, a special teachers' meeting was held, and the Principal stood up to speak first.

"Yesterday's incident was extremely regrettable. In the near future, I expect to receive a reprimand from the Board of Education—"

"If you just shut up about it, you fool, they'll never know," jeered Mr. Adachi, making sure that the Principal could hear.

"Now, I've tried very hard to run this school democratically. I've valued all of your opinions, and as much as possible, I've refrained from expressing my own—"

"That's the problem," heckled Mr. Adachi.

"I feel I've been repaid with a stab in the back."

The Principal rarely spoke so harshly, and the Assistant Principal and Mr. Yamauchi began to feel quite small.

"Now about Minako Ito, the girl in Ms. Kotani's class who was the cause of all this trouble. I permitted Miss Ito to join Ms.

Kotani's class because I was moved by Ms. Kotani's enthusiasm, but since Miss Ito has now been the center of several incidents, I feel that I have no alternative but to reconsider my decision. Of course, I would like to hear sufficiently from Ms. Kotani, but I would also like to hear from all of you."

Mr. Kusage, the head teacher for the first grade, raised his hand.

"The problem is with one of the first-grade classes, so I feel partly responsible, but I think the Principal has something to reflect on, too. When the school decided to take on Miss Ito, the procedures that were followed were not very—"

"It has nothing to do with procedures," jeered Mr. Adachi.

Mr. Kusage immediately turned and faced him.

"Mr. Adachi, I don't appreciate your heckling other people when they're in the middle of speaking. I respect your educational practices, but I don't at all like your gangsterish attitude. Please stop it, or even your good points will be misunderstood."

Mr. Kusage's comment was met with a round of applause, so it was obvious that the offhand remarks had incurred quite a bit of ill feeling. When Mr. Adachi dropped his head into his hands, several teachers broke out laughing, and the applause grew louder. Even Mr. Orihashi and Mr. Ota gleefully joined in.

"When it was decided to let Miss Ito enroll at this school," Mr. Kusage continued, "the only ones that knew about it were the Principal, the Assistant Principal, and Ms. Kotani. It wasn't discussed amongst the first-grade teachers, nor was the issue taken up at a teachers' meeting. No one knew anything about it. I think that contributed to this recent incident. If Minako's case had been discussed ahead of time, and everyone knew about her situation, the problem yesterday might never have occurred."

Ms. Kotani had to agree with him. That was something that hadn't crossed her mind.

"Mr. Kusage's opinion is perfectly reasonable, and I agree with him," responded Mr. Orihashi. "But for that approach to work, each and every teacher has to have a certain understanding about children with disabilities. In a public place like this, everyone will *say* that the education of the mentally handicapped is important, but not everyone *feels* that way, do they? Some teachers call such children 'heavy baggage,' and other teachers say they've struck out when they end up with such a child in their class. And they don't even bat an eye."

Mr. Orihashi hit on a real sore spot.

"Just a moment ago, I referred to a 'certain understanding,' and what I meant by that was that even if you don't know a lot about disabled children, at the very least, you need to be willing to share their hardships. But at a school where some teachers think of such children as being 'baggage,' you have to wonder whether in the final analysis, Mr. Kusage's comment isn't just a whitewashing of the problem."

Mr. Orihashi was rather eloquent today.

Ms. Murano spoke next.

"That was a very impressive speech, but I don't think anyone, including Ms. Kotani, is looking at things from the children's point of view."

Every jaw dropped. Mr. Orihashi had used the exact same words towards her when they were discussing the problem with Koji.

"Mental retardation is an illness, so whenever possible, such children should receive effective medical treatment at a place with the proper facilities. That's why there are special schools for the mentally handicapped. If such children were to attend a regular school like ours, and study with normal children, what would they learn? Nothing. They would only suffer. In Miss Ito's case, she'll be transferring to another school in a month. So after getting used to our school, she's going to have to struggle to readjust to another one. It's cruel to the child."

"Excuse me!" a voice yelled out.

It was Mr. Adachi.

"I'm having a tough time here 'cause I'm not allowed to heckle."

Everyone roared with laughter.

"What Ms. Murano said is wrong, and I would like to correct it," he said, rather highhandedly. It was this way of talking and his merciless attitude that kept others at a distance.

"Ms. Murano spoke about treatment, but if she means the kind of treatment you receive for a stomachache, then she's either mixed up or just plain ignorant. That the cells of the cerebrum, which is to say, nerve cells, do not regenerate is a fact that any junior high school student is aware of, and it is this fact that makes the education of the mentally handicapped different from other kinds of education.

"Ms. Murano threw the question 'What will they learn?' at us. But did you know that this attitude has been criticized as one of the most dangerous attitudes in the field of education for the mentally handicapped? There's an old nun, who spent her entire life working with the mentally handicapped at the renowned Bethel Institute in Bielefeld, Germany, and she said something like this: 'It sounds rational to do what's effective, and to stop doing what's ineffective, but it would be a mistake to apply this to how human beings should live their lives. These children live each and every day. And it's important that they lead lives that for them are joyful and meaningful. This, too, should be one of our aims.' Ms. Murano, we teachers should carefully digest the true meaning of these words. I'm sure Ms. Kotani has never heard them, but hasn't her behavior captured the true spirit of what they really mean?"

Ms. Murano could say nothing in return.

"Since yesterday, Ms. Kotani has been crying and crying, but what does she have to cry about? We should all be urging her to stop crying. In the Bethel homes that I just referred to, the unemployed, the poor, and juvenile delinquents also work as volunteers. We often refer to the mentally retarded as being disadvantaged, but if all human beings have things they must struggle with, then everyone is disadvantaged.

"Ms. Kotani has been having a tough time with Tetsuzo Usui, whom you all know. It's been an extremely painful struggle for her, but with great anguish she has step-by-step moved closer to Tetsuzo's heart. To Ms. Kotani, it doesn't matter if someone is a problem child, mentally disabled, or a teacher: they are all suffering human beings. Today, before you return home, I'd like you to take a look behind the west wing, where you'll find two little sculptures. They are truly wonderful and uplifting creations. Tetsuzo, the problem child, worked together with Minako Ito, the mentally disabled child, to make these inspiring creations. You probably won't believe they could have made them.

"The children in Ms. Kotani's class have warmly accepted Minako, who is called mentally disabled, and Tetsuzo, who is labeled a problem child behind his back. And in learning to live more fully together, they have all, including Ms. Kotani, allowed themselves to get a little dirty. The living proof of this fact can be found in those two sculptures. I respect Ms. Kotani for what she has done. And I want to gently encourage her by saying, 'Don't cry, Ms. Kotani.'"

Mr. Adachi sat down and a hushed silence fell over the room.

15. We Live Only to Say Goodbye

Minako was drawing a picture. First, the student on Minako duty would dab her finger with red, blue, or yellow paint. Then, Minako would run her finger along the large piece of drawing paper, and a colorful and vibrant line would appear. The students called this "action painting," and since there were no rules, it was the perfect activity for a child like Minako. Whenever she was doing one of these pictures, she became extremely animated.

"I'm happy for you, Minako," said Ms. Kotani.

She couldn't imagine how things would have turned out if Mr. Adachi hadn't spoken out at the teachers' meeting. But now Minako was an indispensable part of the class.

The class had changed considerably since Minako's arrival. During the first semester, the students were always telling on one another, but they seldom did that now. They had become more active, and Ms. Kotani became keenly aware that teachers have to take action for students to change. She bashfully admitted to herself that she had changed, too.

It saddened Ms. Kotani that they'd soon have to say goodbye to Minako, and she wondered how they'd ever get along without her. She wished that Minako could stay with them forever.

"Ms. Kotani, aren't we gonna use the lunch cart anymore?" asked Terue.

"No, it's more trouble than it's worth."

The lunch cart was for carrying the large milk can up and

down the aisles so that the milk could be ladled out into the student's cups, but since the classroom was small, the cart often knocked into the desks, and the milk often spilt. The cart turned out to be rather inconvenient, so they had stopped using it.

"Well, then, can we use it for something else?"

"Sure, but what are you going to use it for?"

"We're gonna make a little car for Minako."

"Really?"

"Is that okay?"

"Yes, of course."

Ms. Kotani was intrigued. She kept an eye out and noticed that the students spent all their recesses coloring the mahogany cart. At first, they tried pastel crayons, but the colors didn't show up over the wood, so halfway through, they switched to paint, undiluted with water. They carefully painted one small section at a time, and created various patterns and designs.

"Hey, I didn't get my turn yet!" yelled some students, urging the previous student to stop.

"Sixty, sixty-one, sixty-two, sixty-three . . ." they counted, obviously having established a time limit of one or two hundred per student. Ms. Kotani couldn't help smiling.

"What a pretty cart!" she said.

"Do you really think so?"

"Absolutely. It looks like one of those colorful buses they have in Iran or Pakistan. I bet it's a lot of fun riding a cart like this."

"We're giving Minako rides on it."

"I'd like to go for a ride, too."

"Adults aren't allowed. It'll break."

The cart had taken about three days to complete, and now it looked like a bouquet of flowers. As soon as it was finished, the students took Minako for a test run. When the cart started to move, Minako squealed in delight. She rocked her body back and forth gleefully and began flapping her arms like a bird.

Riding the cart soon became Minako's favorite activity. She had also taken a mysterious fancy to umbrellas, and even when it wasn't raining, she frequently held one over her head. The school's spare umbrellas were yellow, and nothing pleased Minako more than to ride under one of the yellow umbrellas in her cart. The color went well with the red and blue cart.

During class, the students on Minako duty pulled the cart, and Minako rumbled around the classroom noisily. The other students ignored the distraction and listened attentively to their teacher.

The second round of Minako duty started, and this time, Michiko was paired up with Junichi. During lunch, there was a minor incident. The menu for that day was whale meat stew. Since it is served cold, Minako soon put down her spoon and started grabbing it with her hands.

"No!" Michiko yelled, slapping Minako on the hand.

Not having any choice, Minako went back to eating with her spoon.

"Hey, she hit Minako!" taunted Bunji, who was sitting nearby. "She can't do that!"

Ms. Kotani picked up on the incident to initiate the third class discussion concerning Minako.

"When Minako does something bad," said Junichi, "we should let her know. I know everybody likes her, but I think it's a mistake to let her do whatever she wants. Don't you agree?"

"If she doesn't practice," added Michiko, "she'll never improve. It might not bother us if she keeps doin' bad stuff, but then Minako won't be able to get smart. I figure if she studies like the rest of us, she'll get smarter. What do you think, Ms. Kotani?"

Ms. Kotani was especially surprised that the rest of the class agreed with these opinions.

"You guys are really something," said Ms. Kotani. "As a matter of fact, Minako will soon be going to a school for the handicapped, where she'll be practicing all kinds of stuff. She might have a tough time, but I'm sure your idea will come in handy. Isn't that right, Minako?"

Minako giggled and swung from Ms. Kotani's hand.

A couple of days later, Minako had to stay home with a case of tonsillitis. With so little time left, even a day or two's loss was a bitter pill to swallow. Ms. Kotani was disheartened, and the students seemed to lose spirit, too. Some of them rode the vacated cart for a while, but such play had lost its appeal, and they soon dismounted in disillusionment. The cart's bright colors now seemed drab and gloomy.

Ms. Kotani stopped by Minako's house on her way home from school.

"Has she been sleeping?"

"Pretty much. But Junichi and Michiko just came by to pay her a visit, so they're in there having a good time."

"Really? They're here now?"

"That's right. And you know what else?"

Minako's mother lowered her voice to a whisper.

"Junichi's mother just came by and said she wanted to apologize. She said that after reading your newsletter, she's come to understand your point of view, and that more than anything else, she's been really surprised by the change that's come over her son. When he was sitting next to Minako, she had told him to ask you to change his seat, but Junichi told her that he didn't want to. She asked him why he would want to keep getting his stuff torn up, and he said that if he didn't take care of Minako, she would only end up tearing up everybody else's stuff. She said that her son's comment made her feel as if *she* were the child. I thought she sounded very sincere."

"Is that right?" said Ms. Kotani, feeling warm inside.

When Ms. Kotani entered the room, Minako was sitting on her futon, and Junichi and Michiko were lying on their stomachs in front of her. They were folding origami together, but Minako's role was limited to lining up the completed figures.

"Junichi, Michiko, thanks for your help."

"Oh, it's Ms. Kotani," they said, getting up.

"Minako, how are you feeling?" asked Ms. Kotani. Minako burst into smiles and came over to take Ms. Kotani's hand.

"Oh, Minako! You've got a high fever!"

"Yes, she does," said Minako's mother. "I don't know why it is, but a fever doesn't seem to bother her. She's like this even when it goes up to a 101 or 102."

"She's the same as always, Ms. Kotani," said Michiko.

"But if she plays too long, she won't get better, so let's get going pretty soon, okay?"

It pained Ms. Kotani that she would have to force these children to experience the sorrow of separation, and she wondered if she hadn't been cruel in bringing them together.

That evening, Ms. Kotani had a dream.

She was on the beach of a distant sea, perhaps with a coral reef nearby. The choppy white waves could be seen in the offing, and she could faintly hear the sound of the waves, beating softly like the wings of a dragonfly. The pure white sand, undulating gently, appeared out of the waves, and the cobalt blue ocean shone like the eyes of a maiden, deep and kind. A green vine reached out with its tendrils to the beach, and some pink morning glories, turned up towards the heavens like trumpets, were playing a sweet melody. Where was she? Two red crabs ran away, and Ms. Kotani chased after them. *You can't fool me! You're Minako. And you're Tetsuzo. Thought you could trick me by turn-*

ing yourselves into crabs? Well, I'm not falling for that one. Hey, get back here! She ran after them, her hair fluttering behind her. *Hey, that's no fair! You can't run into the ocean!* She tried to head them off, but the crabs laughed and scurried away. *Now you've done it, you bad boy and bad girl. I'm mad, and I've run out of patience.* Ms. Kotani ran along the beach. Minako and Tetsuzo were naked and digging in the sand. *Ha, ha, now I got you.* Minako twisted out of her reach and ran away. Tetsuzo shrieked with laughter and slipped through her arms. Then he put out his arms, and ran away like a bird. *Vroooom*, he said, pretending to be an airplane. Teasing her, he ran away. *You know how to talk! How dare you try to fool me!* Minako's shrill laughter rang in her ears. The children ran, and Ms. Kotani ran after them. *Still plan on running out into the ocean, huh? You really are bad. Well, go ahead. I can swim, so run wherever you like.* Mr. Baku was sitting on a rock playing his cello, and the children jumped up with him. Minako laughed in her high-pitched voice, and Tetsuzo cuddled up against his grandfather, who continued to play. Mr. Baku's eyes were gentle, and he had a big smile. *That's mean! You made me run all this way for nothing.* Mr. Baku took the children by the hand and started to walk away. *Mr. Baku! Wait! I want to go, too!* The sound of the waves grew louder. *Wait! I said wait!* The waves of the ocean surged higher. *What's wrong, Tetsuzo? Don't leave me! Minako, look over here! Mr. Baku! Mr. Baku! Don't leave me! Tetsuzo! Minako!*

Ms. Kotani woke up crying. It was only a dream, but she had shed actual tears. It embarrassed her to have cried over a dream like a child.

The day to say goodbye to Minako finally arrived, and Ms. Kotani did her best to act the same as always. During the noon recess, Minako's parents and grandmother came to the school. They had to go to the new school to take care of some paperwork, so they decided to take Minako home before lunch.

Minako's parents thanked Ms. Kotani, and Minako's mother and grandmother started crying. Ms. Kotani smiled in appreciation. Minako's parents also expressed their thanks to the students.

"Don't mention it!" one of the students yelled as a joke.

Everyone laughed, and Ms. Kotani felt relieved. She wanted the parting with Minako to be as casual as possible, and the laughter was a big help.

The school lunches had already been prepared, but the entire class decided to see Minako off at the gate. Minako was thrilled to be surrounded by all her classmates. She walked in her swaying way, and let out a peal of laughter.

"Minako's in a good mood today, isn't she?" said Takeshi. And then, with a confused look, he added, "Even though she won't be in our class anymore."

At the front gate, the students started calling out.

"Goodbye, Minako!"

Minako giggled happily, and her grandmother bowed many

times in appreciation.

"Come and see us again!"

"Your cart will be waiting for you!"

"Goodbye, Minako!"

Everyone waved goodbye, and Minako laughed even louder. The students didn't stop waving until Minako was completely out of sight.

After they saw Minako off, everyone returned to the classroom to eat. It was usually noisy during lunchtime, but hardly anyone spoke today. A hush fell over the classroom.

Ms. Kotani noticed that Junichi wasn't eating.

"Junichi, what's wrong? Aren't you going to eat your lunch?"

Junichi looked at her with wistful regret. His cheeks started to quiver, and his eyes instantly filled with tears. As if pleading for something, he looked over to Michiko, who was sitting next to him. Then he looked to Takeshi. And then again, he looked at Ms. Kotani. It happened very fast, but it seemed like an eternity. Ms. Kotani quickly turned away from them, and her shoulders started to heave violently. Every student in the class knew that their teacher was crying. The tears flowed down Junichi's cheeks. Michiko, who had been trying to control herself, started to weep loudly. Terue sobbed convulsively. Takeshi sat with his head down. With faces that were sad and chilly, the students gazed down at their cold lunches.

16. The Fly Professor's Research

Ms. Kotani and Tetsuzo had been staring fixedly at the three beakers for quite some time now. For the first time since beginning their fly research, they had a difference of opinion.

Tetsuzo had made great strides in his research. He had been collecting and raising flies for a long time, and using the many pictures that he had drawn, it didn't take long to classify and categorize them. They started with research on the feeding habits of flies, proceeded to research on their life cycle, and then began researching their spawning habits. This research would also show them where to expect outbreaks of flies, so the data was extremely valuable.

As for what flies eat, they performed experiments with every species that Tetsuzo was raising and made a chart listing each fly's favorite foods. Blowflies, green bottle flies, and flesh flies seemed to prefer animal matter, while houseflies seemed to prefer vegetable matter. Tetsuzo's chart turned up some interesting facts. For example, they discovered that although flesh flies do, as their name would suggest, feed on animal matter, they also feed on tree sap. They also did an experiment to determine whether cheese flies do in fact like cheese, and they discovered that while they will swarm to cheese, they are equally attracted to dried fish, so that you couldn't really say they were partial to cheese.

Research on the fly's life cycle was rather simple for Tetsuzo. Since most flies mature from egg to adult fly (or imago) in about twenty days, it was rather easy to observe them. The number of days to maturity varied slightly according to species, but most eggs took about a day to hatch into maggots, which then shed their skin twice before turning into pupas. Tetsuzo's observations showed that this period lasted from six to ten days for houseflies, from seven to nine days for flesh flies and blowflies, and approximately twelve days for green bottle flies.

Pupas normally burrowed into the ground, but when that was impossible, they burrowed into whatever was available. Since Tetsuzo raised his flies in jars, Ms. Kotani had suspected that he was ignorant of this fact, but when she noticed that he brought back more pupas than adults when collecting new samples, she realized that she had underestimated him.

According to Tetsuzo's observations, the period as pupa lasted from four to eleven days for houseflies; from twelve to fifteen days for flesh flies, blowflies, and little house flies; and approximately ten days for green bottle flies. Fruit flies took only about ten days to mature from egg to adult, which was about twice as fast as most other flies.

As for how long flies live, Tetsuzo's test results were unfortunately rather inconsistent, so they couldn't know for sure. Kinjishi II, the fly that replaced the Kinjishi that Bunji had mistakenly fed to the frogs, was already two months old, and showed no signs of kicking off soon. Most flies, however, died within two months.

Flesh flies don't lay their eggs; rather, the eggs hatch inside the mother's body and come out as maggots. Ms. Kotani first learned this from Tetsuzo's research.

A fly's spawning place was generally determined by species, but this information was difficult for Tetsuzo to acquire. Unlike other experiments, which could be done in a jar, this one required a lot of exploring. Ms. Kotani helped when she could. Nothing was too dirty for Tetsuzo, and he didn't hesitate to dig through garbage or a compost heap. When he was examining a dead mouse, Ms. Kotani couldn't stand to get close but instead watched in suspense from afar. She took Tetsuzo to pickle shops, steamed fish paste shops, fish shops, bakeries, and other places with flies, and like a famous detective, he tracked down their spawning places.

Ms. Kotani had made many friends in the market area, and these connections came in handy. Normally, if you went into a restaurant and asked if they had any flies, you would end up getting clobbered.

The top five spawning places were as follows: trash dumps, bathrooms, compost heaps (piles of manure, straw, grass, or fallen leaves), animal carcasses (especially fish, insects, and other small animals), and pickling tubs.

Sometimes, Tetsuzo could determine the species just by looking at the eggs. For example, he could identify the eggs of green bottle flies from their reddish color, and the eggs of houseflies and false stable flies by their size. When he wasn't sure of the species, he brought the eggs home and waited for them to hatch.

In this way, he gradually charted their spawning places, and they learned that spawning places varied by species.

Ms. Kotani couldn't understand why they never found the maggots of houseflies or green bottle flies in the bathroom, even though the maggots of false stable flies, little houseflies, blowflies, and flesh flies were common.

"Houseflies are often in bathrooms, right?" she asked Tetsuzo. "And they feed on human excrement, right? So if they're so closely related to the bathroom, why don't we ever find any of their maggots in there?"

Tetsuzo tilted his head, which meant he really didn't know. Even when he didn't speak, Ms. Kotani's ability to communicate with him had greatly improved. From the movement of his eyes or some other slight movement, she could usually determine what he was thinking. For his part, Tetsuzo had begun speaking a bit more, saying "wrong," "no way," and of course the names of his flies.

"Tetsuzo, you've drawn pictures of the flies, but you haven't drawn pictures of the maggots, right? Well, how about drawing some detailed pictures of all the maggots? We might learn something."

A couple of days later, Ms. Kotani took a glimpse of some of the completed drawings, and the mystery was solved.

"Tetsuzo, there's a little thing sticking out of the rear of some of the maggots, right? Do you know what it's for?"

Tetsuzo shook his head.

"Well, do you know which maggots have one and which don't?"

He nodded.

"Which flies don't have them?"

"Houseflies and green bottle flies."

"Just as I suspected," she said. "Those are the flies that don't have any maggots in the bathroom. Tetsuzo, this thing sticking out is called a stoma, and maggots use it to breathe. Those that have one can survive in dirty places like bathrooms, but those that don't end up drowning to death."

Ms. Kotani was excited at her discovery.

"That's it, Tetsuzo!" she said. "We've solved the mystery of why houseflies and green bottle flies don't have any maggots in the bathroom."

Tetsuzo's eyes were shining, too, and they immediately set up an experiment. First, they heated up some flour and water into a gooey paste. Then, they poured some of the paste into a beaker, and added both kinds of maggots, those with and those without the stoma. The result was as Ms. Kotani had expected: only maggots with the stoma survived. It was through such research on the breeding habits of flies that Tetsuzo would soon bring great credit to himself.

Tetsuzo and Ms. Kotani were now gazing at three beakers: one with sugar, one with sugar-water, and one with water. The sugar-water and water were soaked in cotton, so that the flies would have a place to land.

They had agreed that a fly relies on its sense of smell to find food, but they disagreed about whether water had a scent or not. Tetsuzo said it did, and Ms. Kotani said it didn't. If water had a scent, more flies would go to the beakers with water or sugar-water than to the beaker with only sugar.

They gazed at the beakers in anticipation.

"Oh!" uttered Ms. Kotani. The first fly had stopped at the beaker with sugar-water.

Ms. Kotani looked disappointed, but Tetsuzo just kept staring at the beakers. The second fly stopped at the beaker with water, but quickly moved to the one with sugar-water. It took some time before the next two flies arrived, but after that, they came in one after another. Most of the flies went to the beaker with sugar-water. Quite a few stopped at the beaker with water, but then they usually moved to one of the other two beakers. Few flies flew straight to the beaker with sugar.

"Well, that figures," said Ms. Kotani, smiling. "You were right, and I was wrong. What a pity!"

As they moved further into autumn, Tetsuzo had to hurry his research along. Once it got too cold, his work would have to come to a halt. Flies were not equally active during all seasons of the year. Blowflies and false stable flies completely disappear in mid-summer, and green bottle flies become extremely rare in autumn. The only reason that Tetsuzo had been able to research such a large number of species was that he was breeding them himself. If he had relied on collecting them, he certainly would not have met with such success.

Tetsuzo's research had a subtle effect on his attitude towards flies. Previously, his flies were his pets, and he played with them as you would play with a cat. He only collected flies that he fancied, and he seemed to enjoy raising them. But once he started his observations, he became rather dispassionate. Sometimes they had to thin out a fly population or do an experiment that caused some flies to die, but he didn't get emotional. In the past, if Ms. Kotani had tried to do an experiment like the one with the maggots, she would have ended up having a raving Tetsuzo scratching her face again.

Tetsuzo had started using tweezers for handling flies and maggots. When moving a lot of them, he sometimes fell back into the bad habit of grabbing them with his hands, but Ms. Kotani could see that he tried his best to avoid touching them.

Sometimes he used the alcohol or creosote lotion that Ms. Kotani had given him. He kept new flies that he collected from outside separate from flies that he had raised from birth, but when he had to touch both of them for an experiment, he always used the disinfectant. Ms. Kotani couldn't help laughing when she saw him wiping alcohol on Kinjishi II.

"Tetsuzo," she warned, "flies that don't have any bacteria get weak and die."

After that, he stopped doing it.

Tetsuzo's fly research, then, was proceeding smoothly, but Ms. Kotani had other worries. As far as she was concerned, the research wasn't complete until Tetsuzo was able to write well.

Shortly after Minako transferred, Ms. Kotani initiated the "morning diary" project. She had no intention of making things easy on herself, and the time spent struggling with Minako was now spent on the diaries. Each day, for about forty minutes before school started, she and her students wrote in their diaries. By responding to what her students wrote, she was able to keep up a conversation with each of them. Writing a diary doesn't sound like much, but it was demanding work for Ms. Kotani and her students.

On the first day of the diaries, Tetsuzo wrote "green bottle fly, Kinjishi." On the second day, he wrote "housefly, krap." And on the third day, he wrote, "fruit fly, alkahall." Ms. Kotani responded by writing all kinds of things about flies, Mr. Baku, and other unrelated matters. It would have been easy to correct his spelling or to show him how to write a proper sentence, such as "Fruit flies like alcohol," but Ms. Kotani never did that. She had faith in him.

There is an old proverb that says, "Art holds fast when all else is lost," and in the most unbelievable of circumstances, Tetsuzo distinguished himself and proved this saying true.

One day, Ms. Kotani received a phone call from a ham factory in the school district.

"This probably sounds strange, but we heard that you were doing research on flies. . . ."

"Actually, it's one of my students."

"Well, the reason I'm calling, and this is just between you and me, is that we've been having a hard time with an unusual number of flies. This is cutting into our business, so it's really got us in a fix."

That certainly was true. A ham factory with flies would soon be out of business.

"We've been extremely careful about how we handle the meat, and we've been conscientious about disposing of waste and cleaning the factory, so we have no idea what's causing the problem. Would you be willing to come out to the factory and see what you can do?"

Ms. Kotani wasn't sure how to respond. She wasn't an expert, and she didn't think she'd be able to solve the problem.

"Have you talked to the Health Department?"

"Yes, we have, and we've done everything they suggested, but we still have just as many flies as before . . ."

She figured it wouldn't hurt to take Tetsuzo out and have a look, and even if they didn't succeed, they had nothing to lose. Who knows? Maybe Tetsuzo would find something.

The person from the factory was thrilled when Ms. Kotani agreed.

A big foreign car pulled up in front of the school, and the students started screaming and yelling in excitement. When Ms. Kotani and Tetsuzo boarded, their escort from the factory made a strange face.

"This is the person doing research on flies?"

"That's right," Ms. Kotani answered nonchalantly.

His expression grew even more incredulous, but she could hardly blame him for his reaction.

They were conducted to a splendid reception room, where they were brought tea and cake. After that, they were given a tour of the factory, which turned out to be extremely clean. Ms. Kotani couldn't imagine why they had any flies.

"Strange, isn't it, Tetsuzo?"

Tetsuzo looked puzzled, too. They put their full stock of knowledge about flies into action, but they couldn't figure out the cause.

"Where do you have a lot of flies?" Ms. Kotani asked.

They were guided to where the flies were said to be most numerous, and indeed, there were swarms of them.

"Houseflies!" Tetsuzo screamed.

There was a note of incredulity in his voice, and Ms. Kotani soon realized what he meant. Since they were in a meat factory, you would have expected to see green bottle flies or flesh files, and it was strange that there were only houseflies.

"Weird, isn't it, Tetsuzo?"

All of a sudden, Tetsuzo dashed off and scaled the wall that surrounded the factory. Before long, they could hear him yell.

"That's it!"

A ladder was brought over, and Ms. Kotani and the man from the factory climbed up and had a look. There was a rice field, and along the edge of the road, six huge compost heaps. The riddle was solved.

"There's your problem," said Ms. Kotani. "Houseflies lay their eggs in compost, and since you only have houseflies, I'm absolutely certain that those compost heaps are the source."

About a week later, the school received an expression of the factory's appreciation in the form of an addition to the menu. That day, sausages were on every lunch tray. Not long afterwards, the reason was broadcast to the entire school, and Tetsuzo became an instant hero. The hero himself, however, acted as if it weren't his concern.

"Art holds fast when all else is lost." Ms. Kotani reflected on the meaning of that proverb, and smiled in spite of herself. More than anything else, she was happy that Tetsuzo had spoken in a loud voice for the first time.

17. The Red Chicks

A crowd had formed at the front of the train station, but Ms. Kotani was in a hurry to get home, so she tried to avoid it. As she was squeezing past, she noticed a two- or three-year old boy, blubbering like a baby. His mother was coaxing him to leave, but he refused to budge.

Ms. Kotani peeked inside the crowd. Red chicks and blue chicks were chirping and jostling about inside a cardboard box. Some green turtles, about two inches long, were crawling around in a washbowl. The boy was obviously crying for one or the other of them, so Ms. Kotani assumed that such pets were popular. But why were the chicks red? And who ever heard of blue chicks? She looked more closely and noticed that they had been dyed, for there were some bald spots, where lonely yellow hairs peeked out along the edges. The sight revolted her.

The boy finally stopped his blubbering, but then he pulled his mother's hand and pushed into the crowd. His mother handed the man some money, and one of each colored chick was packed away into a little box. When the box was handed to the boy, he grinned with satisfaction. Ms. Kotani found his grin repulsive. Then she suddenly thought of her husband.

Several months earlier, she and her husband had gone to Saidaiji Temple, which was charming in the summer rain.

"We're lucky to see Saidaiji in the rain," said Ms. Kotani breezily. "Look at that! The green looks like it's going to just melt off the trees."

They talked about the earthen walls and argued about the beauty of the temple's bamboo. When they reached the main hall, their interests diverged. Ms. Kotani was still a fan of Zenzai Doji.

"So how have I done?" she asked the statue, with a small degree of confidence. "Have I become a bit more beautiful?"

Her husband preferred the temple's main statue of Buddha. He said that the lines of its robes had a celestial beauty.

"Now that you mention it," said Ms. Kotani, "he is rather handsome." The temple priest certainly would have frowned if he had heard that.

"How about I take you to a secret place?" she asked her husband.

They went past the pagoda remains to the right until they reached a small pond. The many bushes in the area discouraged people from approaching. Lining the edge of the pond were small stone statues of Buddha. Ms. Kotani often came here for the rustic scenery.

"The scenery's really nice, don't you think?"

"Yeh," her husband replied tersely.

"The stone Buddhas are interesting," she said. "They're not all puffed up with dignity. They look like regular guys and ladies that you'd meet on the street."

She turned and faced her husband. He was standing in a daze, and his eyes were vacant. He might have been thinking about something, but his mouth was hanging open. Ms. Kotani had never seen him look like that before, and it made her feel creepy, as if she had suddenly seen a ghost.

Shortly after the visit to Saidaiji Temple, her husband's friend started paying them frequent visits, apparently to discuss work. Ms. Kotani was usually tired when she got home, but she tried hard to receive their guest with a smile, usually by recalling something that Mr. Adachi or Mr. Orihashi had said to help her pull through. The frequent visits continued for a while.

"I'd like to invest in my friend's business," her husband said one day. "And I was wondering if I could use the land your father gave us as collateral on a loan?" He also said that he was going to quit his current job and manage the business jointly with his friend.

"Sure, that would be okay," answered Ms. Kotani. Her feeling was that even if he didn't succeed, it was better to live passionately than to end up being one of those spiritless businessmen whose only goal in life was to own a house.

Her husband became a manager of the company just around the time that Minako joined her class. A party celebrating his new move was held at their house. After the typical words of praise and the endless discussions about various male diversions, the party finally came to an end. Her husband looked completely exhausted. As she was laying out the futons, she tried to cheer him up.

"You really have it rough, too," she said.

Suddenly, he took her in his arms.

"I want to make things easier for you," he whispered. "Just be a little more patient, okay? You won't have to work much longer."

Ms. Kotani was thrown for a loop. She couldn't believe he could make such a suggestion, but to avoid hurting his feelings, she didn't say anything.

The red chicks chirped the same as the blue chicks, and they both undoubtedly sounded the same as natural yellow ones. When Ms. Kotani considered that their voices could not be dyed, the chirping began to sound like a passionate cry of resistance. She wondered what it meant to be alive. And she wondered what it meant to live with someone.

When she got home, her husband was standing in the doorway, his face pale and his hands shaking.

"We've had some trouble," he said, as soon as she walked through the door.

"What happened?"

"Can't you tell? We've been burglarized!"

Sure enough, the house was full of policemen, and the living room had been ransacked. A man dressed in white was dusting powder all over the bureau. No doubt, he was looking for the fingerprints of the burglar. Before she knew it, her own fingers were being pressed to an inkpad, too.

"Why do I have to be fingerprinted?"

"To distinguish them from the culprit's," answered the young police officer.

Every little thing that was stolen had to be reported. Ms. Kotani could easily recall the larger items, but she honestly wasn't sure about the smaller ones. Her husband, who was sitting beside her, rattled off the names of the missing articles for her. Inwardly, she was surprised. In most households, the wife was the expert, but in their home, it was the other way around. She ludicrously started thinking how the guy really had stolen quite a bit.

"Do you work, too?" the officer asked.

"Yes, I do."

"Two-income families need to be especially careful, you know."

"Yes."

Ms. Kotani felt silly for replying to his stupid comment. What were they supposed to be careful about? They always locked up the house before going out, so what more were they supposed to do? And why were two-income families supposed to be especially careful? Instead of accusing them, the officer should have been reassuring them.

Ms. Kotani's husband acted as if the police were doing them a great favor. This annoyed her, and she yanked his shirt to get him to stop.

"Boy, they really cleaned us out, didn't they?" she said, once the police were gone. She was trying to be cheerful, because she couldn't stand to see their home life grow somber over such a thing.

"Yeh, right," said her husband.

He couldn't complain because he was a man, but Ms. Kotani knew that he was annoyed. Just to make sure, he kept asking her about bankbooks and other documents whose loss they would have to report in order to avoid additional damage.

"It's a shame I lost the pearl brooch you gave me," she said, testing him. As if on cue, he started listing all the items that they had lost, and she secretly regretted having said anything.

Three days later, the culprit was all too easily arrested.

They were having dinner when the doorbell rang, and Ms. Kotani went to answer it. At the door were a detective, several police officers, and a short, pathetic-looking man with a handcuff attached to his right hand. Ms. Kotani was taken aback.

"We're sorry to bother you at night, ma'am, but he claims to have hidden some of the stolen property in the ceiling. Would you let us inspect the area?"

"Sure, go ahead."

Ms. Kotani felt like she was in a television drama. The handcuff on the man's wrist glimmered ominously, and she thought she was going to faint.

The ceiling panel was easily removed. Though it was her own home, Ms. Kotani didn't know that this could be done. Several small but expensive items soon appeared, the pearl brooch amongst them.

"Why would he hide them there?" asked her husband, as if talking to himself.

"What? Are you kidding? He probably heard a noise and got

scared," said one of the police officers, with contempt. "This guy's a real wimp, you know." Then he turned to the man, yelled "Boo!" and gave him a poke. Rattled, the man threw himself to the ground and prostrated himself at Ms. Kotani's feet.

"Please forgive me!"

"Oh, it's all right," she said without thinking. The police officers broke out laughing, and Ms. Kotani turned red.

"The property never left your house, so technically we can't say it was stolen. There might be some paper work we need to do, but why don't we just return them to you right now and call it a night?"

Ms. Kotani's husband accepted the articles.

As they were leaving, Ms. Kotani saw the suspect's face for the first time. He looked old and had bleary eyes. He seemed lost and confused. When he lowered his head and turned to go, she gasped. He didn't have a left hand. Maybe he lost it in the war or maybe in a traffic accident. She cringed as she watched him being hauled away.

"That's how it is for some people," said her husband pensively.

Ms. Kotani plopped down on the floor and stared at the pearl brooch, which had just been returned to her. For her, it had lost its glimmer, and owning it felt like a crime.

"Well, it's good you got it back," said her husband. He was only stating the obvious, but Ms. Kotani hated him for saying it.

The next evening, the disposal plant children came to Ms.

Kotani's house. Isao, Yoshikichi, Shiro, and Tokuji were all there.

"Good evening."

Jun and Keiko peeked in, too.

"Good evening, Ms. Kotani."

"What's this? How many of you have come?"

"Everybody."

"Everybody?"

The children trooped into the house, together with Shigeko, Takeo, and Misae.

"Wow, it really is everybody," she said, in surprise. "I guess Tetsuzo's the only one that couldn't make it."

"No, he's here, too, Ms. Kotani."

"Really?" she said, amazed.

"Come on, Tetsuzo," said Isao. "Aren't ya gonna come in?"

Ms. Kotani went outside and found Tetsuzo fidgeting behind the door.

"Oh, Tetsuzo's come, too? I'm so happy. Well, come in, come in." She pulled Tetsuzo's hand, but he was extremely bashful. This was the first time she had ever seen him like this.

The children sat decorously. Their parents must have lectured them about how to behave. They had big smiles on their faces, and it looked like they would break out laughing any second.

Surprised at the commotion, Ms. Kotani's husband appeared from the next room. The children very properly exchanged greetings with him.

"He's your husband?" asked Isao.

"That's right."

"He's really handsome, isn't he?" added Jun.

"You're just saying that."

"No, I'm not! It's the truth!" said Jun, getting uptight.

Her husband said that he was going out for a bath or something and headed to the door. As Ms. Kotani was seeing him off, he made a comment that deeply upset her.

Shigeko said, "The place looks pretty clean for being robbed."

"It was tough cleaning up," replied Ms. Kotani.

Shigeko's comment seemed to be a signal, and the children reached into their bags.

"This is from the parents at the disposal plant," said Isao, handing Ms. Kotani an envelope that read, "A Token of Our Sympathy." A short letter and twenty thousand yen were enclosed.

Dear Ms. Kotani,

We heard you had a bit of an unpleasant experience. We don't think you're the kind of person to fall to pieces over a little burglary, but please hang in there. This is a small token of our sympathy.

"This is for you, too," said Jun, placing a small frog-shaped bank in front of her. He looked embarrassed.

One after another, the children presented her with piggy banks and envelopes. Yoshikichi and some others willingly parted with wooden banks that they had obviously made themselves.

Tetsuzo plunked down a string threaded with dozens of five-yen coins.

Since they all had brought money apparently by previous agreement, it was obvious that they had given the gesture a lot of thought.

"Ms. Kotani, are ya gonna be able to eat?" asked Tokuji. "If ya need to, you can use my money to get some rice."

Now she understood why they were so concerned. If their homes had been robbed, they would have had to go hungry. That was what Tokuji was telling her.

"I'm very touched," she said, expressing her thanks in a tearful voice.

The children said nothing in criticism of the robber. They were only concerned about Ms. Kotani's wellbeing.

"Get rid of them quick!" her husband had told her on his way out. He added that he just couldn't deal with kids, but his initial demand caused her to close her ears to his explanation.

She thought of the chicks, those poor red chirping chicks whose natural down had been soiled and dirtied.

18. Infant Guerrillas

At about three o'clock in the afternoon, Isao and Yoshikichi came running up as fast as they could.

"Tetsuzo!" they yelled, terror-stricken. "Lucky's been caught! The dog catchers got 'im!"

Tetsuzo was taking records on his flies, but he immediately stopped and glanced over at them. When he saw their expressions, he jumped up and dashed off.

"Tetsuzo! Hold on! Wait for us!"

They had no idea that Tetsuzo could run so fast. By the time Isao managed to catch him, they had reached the entrance of the disposal plant.

"Settle down, Tetsutsun," he said, gasping for breath. "What'd ya think you're gonna do all by yourself? You're not dealing with Ms. Kotani. They're not gonna break down cryin' just 'cause you bite 'em."

Isao was trying to scare him into submission, but Tetsuzo struggled to break free from his grip.

"Tetsutsun, listen to me!" yelled Isao, shaking him by the shoulders with all his might. "You're still little, so why don't ya let us handle it, okay? I guarantee we'll get Lucky back for you."

Tetsuzo finally backed down, just as Yoshikichi caught up with them.

"Boy! You guys are fast!" he said, breathing heavily.

"No, you're slow," said Isao, as if he were talking to a fool.

"Now hurry up and round up the guys. Tetsutsun, you, too."

The two boys ran off, and Isao plopped down on the ground. With a serious look, he pondered what to do.

"Did Lucky really get caught?" asked Jun, who came running up first.

"Yeh, he did," answered Isao. "And you're just the guy I wanted to see. Can ya listen to my plan about how to get 'im back?"

Jun was considered the brains of the disposal plant gang, so Isao whispered to him his plan for freeing Lucky.

Before long, everyone was assembled except Shigeko, who was off visiting relatives.

"I'd feel really sad for Tetsuzo if he lost Lucky," said Misae, looking like she was going to cry.

"That's why we're gonna get 'im back, you idiot," said Jun, sounding superior.

"Okay, everybody, gather round," said Isao. First, he assigned them their tasks. Then, he drew a map in the dirt and detailed the plan.

When the discussion was finished, the children scattered off in different directions, and when they reassembled, they each were carrying a weapon. Armed with saws, hammers, crowbars, mallets, and nail pullers, they looked like guerilla fighters heading into battle. If their teachers saw them, they would have had heart attacks.

The children left the disposal plant, and eventually found the dogcatchers working in an alley of the shopping district.

Including the driver, there were three men. On the back of the truck, there was a heavy wooden cage with half-inch thick bars spaced about four inches apart. Behind the bars, seven or eight dogs were yelping piteously.

Isao and his rescue team hid in the shadows and watched the men work. Some of the boys had to struggle to keep Tetsuzo from running out after them. Many of the dogs were howling, but Tetsuzo could make out Lucky's bark.

"Tetsutsun, it's not gonna be much longer," said Tokuji, with sympathy. He had pigeons as pets, so he knew how Tetsuzo was feeling.

"Here they come!" Shiro screamed in a shrill voice.

Driven by one of the dogcatchers, a red dog came racing frantically in their direction. The other dogcatcher was lying in wait, and he closed in with a shiny metal pole, which he held over his head. The dog leapt to avoid him, but the pole moved a split second faster. A white light cut through the air like a flash of lightening. The dog flipped in midair and came crashing down to the ground on his back.

With a practiced hand, the man jerked the shiny pole so that it dug firmly into the dog's neck. The dog squealed in pain, and his bloodshot eyes moved back and forth as if searching for someone to rescue him. The man tightened the grip of the pole even more and lifted the dog into the air. The dog kicked his hind legs violently, but they only flapped futilely in the air. He put his front legs together and moved his body as if to jump, but the pole biting into his neck was tightened still more. The dog writhed in agony. And then, urine and feces began dripping down between his legs.

Isao and Jun turned pale. They held Tetsuzo down by the shoulders, so that he wouldn't bolt out after the dogcatchers.

Had Lucky been captured in the same way? The children couldn't bear to think how Tetsuzo must be feeling.

"Stay calm, Tetsutsun, stay calm," said Isao, sounding a little delirious. He was nervously jiggling his legs, which was a quirk he had when he was excited.

The dog, still hanging from the pole, was tossed into the cage, and with the arrival of the newcomer, the other dogs began yelping louder. The two men pulled out their cigarettes, evidently intending to take a breather.

"Okay, get goin'," ordered Isao, in a low voice. Keiko and Misae stood up.

"Do a good job," said Jun nervously to his sister.

Keiko and Misae held hands tightly, and though they were nervous, they walked with a steady gait. They went right up to the two men who were smoking.

"Hey, mister," said Keiko. "We know where there's a ton of stray dogs."

The men looked at the girls suspiciously. They had never had a child help them before.

"If ya go straight up this road, there's a disposal plant, right? Well, dogs go in there to eat leftover food. It's really easy for 'em, so they've really settled in."

"They're always causin' trouble," added Misae, trying to make the story sound good, "so my mother wants ya to catch 'em."

"We'll show ya the way, so let's go," said Keiko.

"Oh, I don't know," muttered one of the men.

"What'd I wanna lie for?" said Keiko, acting put out. "Somebody comes all this way, and then ya don't even believe 'em? Geez!" She was quite the actress.

"Okay, okay. Sorry. So can you show us where they are?" said the older man.

"Sure, let's go," said Keiko, walking off ahead of them.

The truck started moving. Everything was proceeding as Isao had planned. He and his band followed the truck from behind, being careful to stay out of sight.

Finally, they reached the disposal plant.

"Mister, can ya bring the truck 'round to the back?" Keiko asked. Few people passed behind the disposal plant, so it was the ideal spot for an attack.

"I guess so."

The men brought the truck around as they were told. Up to that point, everything had gone according to plan.

"So where're the dogs?"

"They're inside a pipe."

"There are dogs in a pipe?"

"I guess they feel safe in there," said Keiko, just spitting out whatever popped into her head.

Two of the men went off with the girls, and the third man stayed in the truck smoking his cigarette.

"What's she doin'!" exclaimed Isao, who was watching from his hiding place. "If she leaves a guy behind, we won't be able to do anything! She's so stupid!"

Keiko was frantic about the man staying behind. She knew she had to do something. But what? She racked her brains until her head hurt. Then she turned around and ran up to him.

"Come on, mister," she said. "You gotta come, too."

"What're you talking about? I don't catch dogs. I just drive the truck."

"Yeh, but the pipe's really wide, you know. All you gotta do is stand there, so the dogs can't get by. You can handle that. With just two guys, they're gonna get away. Now, come on, let's go."

Keiko started yanking him by the hand.

"I can't win with this kid," said the man, grudgingly going along with her.

"She did it!" said Isao, jumping for joy. "That's my sister for you."

No one criticized Isao for bragging this time.

Keiko brought the three men to the entrance of the pipe.

"What's this? It's just a sewer pipe."

"We're not going in there, are we?" said the driver, wretchedly.

"There's really a dog in there?"

"What're ya sayin', mister? It's a regular den of stray dogs. It's not like there's only one or two. There's gotta be four or five in there at least. You gotta make some effort. Now, come on!"

Keiko and Misae plunged ahead into the pipe, and the men reluctantly trailed along behind them.

"Boy, it really stinks in here," grumbled one of them.

"There's one! He ran off that way!" yelled Keiko, doing her best to trick them. The men scrambled off to where she pointed, but the sewage pipe was dark and narrow, making it difficult to run.

"Mister! Over there! Over there!"

Huffing and puffing, the men ran and ran.

"You guys are too slow."

"Oh, there he goes!" screamed Misae, getting in on the act.

Meanwhile, Isao and his band were busy. The instant the men disappeared into the pipe, they raised a battle cry, and started their attack on the dog cage. They jumped up onto the back of the truck like grasshoppers and went to work. Their hammers smashed through the top, their crowbars wrenched open the bars, and their saws cut through the sides. Even little Tetsuzo and Koji swung their hammers frantically.

Yoshikichi was considered a lout, but his large body came in handy this time. A hole opened up in the roof of the cage first, and a second later, a gash opened up in the side, too.

"Lucky!" yelled Tetsuzo.

With his tail wagging furiously, Lucky jumped up on Tetsuzo

and started licking his face.

"Lucky! Lucky!" cried out Tetsuzo, hugging his dog.

Isao climbed into the cage through the hole in the roof.

"While we're at it," he said to the dogs, "we might as well set you guys free, too. Now, go on! Get out of here!"

The dogs leapt and romped about joyously. In a few minutes, they were gone. Within another twenty minutes, however, the police had rounded up the disposal plant children as if they had been the escaping stray dogs.

Mr. Adachi and the other homeroom teachers rushed to the police station with the Assistant Principal, who immediately apologized on behalf of the school.

"What kind of education are you giving these kids anyway?" fumed one of the dogcatchers. From the look and smell of their muddy clothes, it was clear that they hadn't had time to change since their plunge into the sewer.

"Who's in charge of this one?" asked the other dogcatcher, giving Keiko a push.

"I am," said Mr. Orihashi, speaking slowly.

"What kind of kid is she?"

"'What kind of kid?' Oh, I don't know . . . I guess she's smart and clever."

"Yeh, she's clever all right."

Fretting and fuming, the man explained how Keiko had tricked them. Mr. Adachi, who was standing at the man's side, had to struggle to keep from laughing.

"She's a real terror."

All the blame was being pinned on Keiko.

The children were lined up in a row from Isao, who was in the sixth grade, to Tetsuzo, who was in the first. Isao was looking off in the other direction with feigned ignorance. Yoshikichi was nonchalantly picking his nose. The only one that seemed even mildly humbled by the experience was Jun. The others seemed completely oblivious of what they had done.

"They haven't reflected on their behavior in the least!" yelled the portly chief of police, protesting partly out of regard for the dogcatchers.

"Koji, hurry up and apologize," fretted Ms. Murano.

"You guys are idiots," put in Mr. Adachi. "If you wanted to get Lucky back, all you had to do was get him vaccinated and get a permit."

"We don't got the money for that," Isao spat back.

"Yeh, I guess you're right," said Mr. Adachi, backing down. Mr. Adachi didn't seem too trustworthy, and you had to wonder if he hadn't prompted Isao's response.

"Take a look at what they did to the truck," said the chief of police, pointing to the courtyard, where it was parked.

"Geez!" chuckled Mr. Adachi. "They did a quite job on that, too." Ms. Kotani poked him in the ribs.

"And that's what they destroyed it with," added the chief of police, pointing to the hammers, saws, and other weapons piled in the corner.

"Give us back our stuff!" ordered Yoshikichi, simplemindedly.

"What are you gonna do about our truck?" retorted one of the dogcatchers.

"How should *I* know?"

"You think you can get away with it that easy, huh?" said the man, getting annoyed.

"You shouldn't have gone stealin' someone's dog without sayin' anything!" screamed Isao.

"You're in the sixth grade, aren't you? Surely, a sixth-grader knows why stray dogs need to be rounded up."

"Lucky's not a stray dog."

"If he's unlicensed, he's a stray."

"You decided that yourself just to suit your own nasty purposes."

"You got a smart-ass answer for everything, don't you?" said the man, faltering.

"To begin with, their way of talking is unacceptable," said the chief of police, shaking his head indignantly.

"This is a school issue."

"Yeh, I guess it is," said Mr. Adachi, as if it had nothing to do with him.

In the end, the children's parents were called in, and it was agreed that they would compensate the men for the broken cage. After an hour-long lecture by the chief of police, the students, parents, and teachers were finally released.

19. An Unfortunate Decision

The next day, Mr. Adachi, Mr. Orihashi, Mr. Ota, and Ms. Kotani visited the disposal plant. The children were gathered at their fort and looked absolutely miserable. They appeared to be in the midst of deliberations.

"So how are my little guerrilla fighters doing?" asked Mr. Adachi. "You look a bit down, but we've brought something to cheer up the troops."

He held out the *taikoyaki* that he had brought, but no one seemed interested.

"This is unusual. I guess you guys really got bawled out there yesterday, huh? So what's wrong, Isao?"

"It's useless," he said, shaking his head.

"What is?"

"Repairin' the cage is gonna cost sixty thousand yen."

"Sixty thousand yen?"

"Yeh."

"That's pretty expensive, huh?"

"It's gonna be years before any of us get an allowance again. I can live with that, but my family's gonna have to go back into debt, so I'm in a real fix."

"Yeh, who wouldn't be?" said Mr. Adachi, with a grave look.

Ms. Kotani had just received help because of the burglary, so it was painful for her to stand by and do nothing.

"We've been tryin' to think of a way to raise the money," said

Isao, looking forlorn. "But makin' money's not all that easy."

"We could ask for donations at the school," said Mr. Ota, "but since you did what you did, I doubt we'd get very much."

"Isao, I'll give you some money from my next paycheck," said Ms. Kotani.

"Don't even think it!" said Mr. Adachi, with a censorious look. "I told you I was hard up with my drinking debts!"

"Sixty thousand yen, huh?" said Mr. Orihashi. "That was a rather costly raid you guys made there. I guess that's what they call a Pyrrhic victory." It was one of his typical comments.

"Come on and eat up. I brought them just for you," said Mr. Adachi, putting out the *taikoyaki* again. "I wonder if we couldn't find a couple more situations like we had at the ham factory the other day. Tetsuzo could make enough all by himself." He sounded as if he were seriously considering putting Tetsuzo to work.

"I just thought of a good idea," burst out Mr. Orihashi. "You got some of those big two-wheeled carts here at the disposal plant, don't you? Well, we could borrow them and be junk collectors. You can make money collecting junk, you know."

"Junk collectors?" said Mr. Ota, not sounding particularly enthralled by the idea.

"Don't make fun. It's not easy work, but we can definitely make some money."

"Yeh, let's do it," said Mr. Adachi, slapping his knee. "How about it, Isao? You'll do anything, right? And you guys will all pitch in, too, won't you?"

The children's eyes gleamed.

"We'll do anything," said Isao, suddenly in good spirits.

It took Mr. Adachi a couple of days to complete all the necessary negotiations. First, he had to convince the disposal plant parents to allow their children's teachers to organize such work. Second, he had to haggle with other junk collectors, who protested that the plan was a violation of their rights. Through his strenuous efforts, these problems were solved. After that, they only had to collect the junk and lug it to a wholesaler.

"So we're gonna do it after all?" said Mr. Ota, unenthusiastically.

"You don't have to if you don't want to," said Mr. Adachi.

"I'll do it, I'll do it," he relented in despair.

The four teachers headed to the disposal plant wearing sweat pants and straw hats for protection from the sun. When they arrived, the children were already waiting for them. They acted like they were going on a field trip or something.

"I've gotta collect trash because of you guys," said Mr. Ota, still complaining.

"Aren't you the one who's always saying that all trades are equally honorable?" scolded Mr. Adachi.

At the front gate of the disposal plant, the four large carts headed off in different directions.

"Do a good job!"

"You, too!"

The children had been divided into four groups. In Ms.

Kotani's group were Jun, his sister Misae, and Tetsuzo. Ms. Kotani stood between the shafts; Jun pulled over his shoulder a rope that was attached to the front bar; and Misae and Tetsuzo pushed from behind. Lucky, wearing a new collar from which dangled a shiny aluminum license, ran circles around them. Ms. Kotani had bought the license with some of her savings.

Since Ms. Kotani was a woman, it was suggested that she join one of the other groups, but she refused. Even one more cart meant that much more money. She had received all of the children's savings after the burglary, so she wanted to repay their kindness.

Passers-by stared at them. Although Ms. Kotani was a married woman, she was still young and easily embarrassed. She kept her head down as she pulled.

"Ms. Kotani, if ya don't yell out anything, nobody's gonna bring out their stuff," said Jun.

"What am I supposed to yell?"

Needless to say, Ms. Kotani had no experience in the junk trade. She never even had a part-time job in her college years, so she was difficult to deal with in situations such as this.

"Cash for trash!" called Jun.

"Oh! I heard that in a comedy routine once."

"It's got nothing to do with comedy. You can say whatever ya want. 'Get rid of your trash!' 'Old newspaper! Old clothes! Anything ya don't need!'"

"Wow, Jun, you're really good. Why don't we leave it to you?"

said Ms. Kotani, cunningly. Jun threw up his hands in despair.

Ms. Kotani's initial enthusiasm had evaporated, and as time passed, she grew more and more discouraged.

"Jun, what are we going to do?"

"What're ya talkin' about, Ms. Kotani? We haven't got anything yet."

Just then, someone called out, "Ms. Kotani, is that you?" She turned around and was greeted by the mother of one of her students.

"Ms. Kotani, what are you doing?"

Ms. Kotani fidgeted in embarrassment.

"Excuse me, ma'am," said Jun, who was standing there. "Do ya got any newspapers, magazines, or old clothes that ya don't need?"

"Oh, you're collecting recyclables? That must be really hard on you, Ms. Kotani. Are you trying to get more books for the library again?"

"Something like that."

The school library had few books, and the PTA had once collected trash in order to buy more.

"I'll go tell the people in my neighborhood."

What a huge relief! Three families brought newspapers, magazines, bottles, and other discarded items.

Jun was ecstatic, and with Tetsuzo and Misae bundling up the newspaper with string, the small group was soon a flurry of activity.

"Jun, can you grab the scale?" They didn't have a proper one, so they had borrowed a bathroom scale from the school. Ms. Kotani weighed the articles, checked the Refuse Purchasing Price List that Mr. Adachi had written out for them, and paid the amount. The mothers made a strange face.

"Isn't it a contribution for the school?"

Not having any choice, Ms. Kotani briefly explained that they were helping a student who had met with a personal misfortune.

"I guess we've got to swallow our pride. Don't we, Jun?"

"Yeh."

"I got a good idea. Why don't we go around to the houses of the kids in my class? From just three houses, we got this much stuff."

The four carts returned to the disposal plant just as it was getting dark, and every cart had a full load.

"Wow! Ms. Kotani's group did a great job, too."

They all had dirty faces, but they were in high spirits. The first day was such a huge success that they didn't notice how exhausted they were. Shiro's mother came out to tell them that dinner had been prepared and that everyone was invited. When Mr. Adachi politely refused, he was told that all the parents had helped out, and that they weren't accepting any refusals.

A lively meal started, and the disposal plant parents popped in one after another. Mr. Baku brought some of his beef stew, which he said had been simmering away all morning. The children stuffed their faces with rice balls, and Mr. Adachi and some other adults enjoyed drinking beer and sake.

"How much do you think we'll get for one cartload?" Mr. Adachi asked Shiro's father.

"Oh, I don't know. I guess yours will fetch four thousand yen or so, and Ms. Kotani's will probably pull in about three thousand."

"Wow! We made that much in just three hours?" said Mr. Adachi, his eyes wide with surprise. "I'm gonna quit teaching and start doing this for a living."

"What're ya talkin' about, Mr. Adachi?" put in Isao, who was listening in. "When we were callin' out for trash, we couldn't hear you at all!"

"Don't say that!" said Mr. Adachi, getting flustered.

"Aha! So you had the same problem that . . ." said Mr. Ota, incriminating himself.

Takeo, who was in Mr. Orihashi's group, started to say something, but Mr. Orihashi hurriedly covered his mouth.

"Aha! I guess you couldn't do it either," said Mr. Adachi, with a grin.

"You're supposed to be men, but you're just a bunch of sissies," said Jun. "You should've heard Ms. Kotani yellin' 'Cash for Trash!' She was great, wasn't she, Misae?"

He poked his sister with his foot, and she nodded with indifference.

"Wow!" said Mr. Adachi and Mr. Orihashi, obviously impressed.

"I'll have to give you more credit," said Mr. Ota, burying his head in his hands.

Ms. Kotani giggled, and when she looked over at Tetsuzo, who was sitting next to Misae, she was in for a surprise. He was actually smiling! The meal was that much fun.

But all good things must come to an end.

The next day, Ms. Kotani heard something that made her skin crawl.

"It's been formally decided that the disposal plant will be moved soon," Mr. Adachi told her when he stopped in to see her during the noon recess. His face was somewhat pale, which was rather unusual for him.

Ms. Kotani was stunned. "To where?"

"To the number three landfill."

"I thought they said that that was unacceptable."

An automated waste disposal plant had been built at the number three landfill, but since it would be possible to build the same kind of modern disposal plant at the number five landfill, they had planned to move Isao and the other children's disposal plant there. According to the plan, that was supposed to be more than two and a half years from now.

"So why are they suddenly changing their minds?"

"I guess the campaigning of the residents near the current plant has been pretty intense."

"But you can't very well be against moving the plant."

"That's true, moving the plant is definitely best. But it's the people living at the plant, especially the children, who will be victimized."

"What do you mean?"

"It'll take them fifty minutes to get to this school."

"Fifty minutes!"

"Of course, you can't expect elementary school kids to make such a long commute, so the decision is to have them change schools. But there's a problem with that, too. It's only a twenty-minute trip, but they'd have to pass through the landfill to get to their new school. Some of those roads are teeming with dump trucks, so it'd be pretty dangerous for the kids."

"You can't have people live in a place like that."

"Exactly. And they're gonna have a tough time living there. It'll take them thirty or forty minutes just to get to the nearest market."

"Couldn't they just find a place for them to live in town?"

"That would be ideal, but then there would be problems with residency rights and compensation. The most economical approach would be to put up some prefab housing near the new disposal plant. Don't you think?"

"How come you know all about this? Judging from how everybody was yesterday, nobody at the disposal plant knows anything about it."

"Well, City Hall knows about it, and they also know that the biggest problem with the move is the kids' commute to school. They want to avoid any problems before they occur, right? Well, they came to our school to feel us out. Just a moment ago, I was called into the Principal's office, and asked if I'd be able to persuade the parents at the plant."

"So did you agree to do it?"

"Who'd agree to such a thing?"

"I'd be so upset if I lost Tetsuzo. It wasn't so long ago that I had to say goodbye to Minako." Ms. Kotani was visibly upset.

"Yeh, I'd really miss them, too," said Mr. Adachi, becoming sentimental.

20. The Humble Samurai

For three days in a row, the four groups returned with their junk carts full, but on the fourth day, the loads became lighter as if by some previous arrangement. The four teachers immediately understood why.

"I guess you guys finished doing the rounds, huh?" said Mr. Adachi.

They had a good laugh about how all of them had gone around to the homes of their students. The first four days had brought in a total of forty-eight thousand yen.

"Just a little bit more. If everyone can get their cart filled up just one more time, we should be all right after tomorrow."

"I'm not too confident, though," said Mr. Ota.

He and Mr. Orihashi exchanged glances and sighed.

"I guess from tomorrow we're gonna have to do the 'Cash for Trash!' routine for real," said Mr. Orihashi.

"I'm not too good at that," said Mr. Ota, looking miserable.

On the fifth day, the four groups set off with a grim resolution.

"Jun, today we're doing cash for trash," said Ms. Kotani, "so I'm really counting on you." She pressed her hands together and pleaded with him.

Ms. Kotani had gotten used to pulling the heavy cart. Sometimes, Tetsuzo came around to the front and pulled with her. The past four days had been an educational experience. She had no idea that physical labor could be so invigorating or that water could taste so incredibly delicious after working up a sweat.

She was also surprised to see how hard the children could work. Children so rarely pitched in to help nowadays, so that when she saw little Misae and Tetsuzo laboring away, she felt that much more affectionate towards them. She couldn't believe that this was the same Tetsuzo that sat staring off into space during class.

Although it was late autumn, the sun glared intensely, and Ms. Kotani and the children were soon perspiring.

"Jun, my skin's not getting dark, is it?"

"Not all that much. Why? Ya worried about it?"

"I'm still young and want to keep my nice complexion."

"Worried your husband might stop lovin' ya, huh?"

"I think you'd make a better husband. I'd marry you if you weren't a kid."

"Oh, I get it. It's a trick. You figure you'll butter me up, and get me to call out for trash."

"No, that's not it at all. It's true. I want to marry you. And I want to marry Tetsuzo. And I want to marry Isao. And I want to . . ."

"Boy, you're shameless."

"Talk to us, too, Ms. Kotani," complained Misae from the back of the cart. "You're only talkin' to my brother."

"Oh, you're just jealous," said Jun, enjoying himself.

Tetsuzo pushed the cart in silence, and Lucky kept busy running off in various directions. Sometimes, he chased after Tetsuzo and barked, but Tetsuzo just ignored him and went on pushing.

"Jun."

"What?"

"Today we're gonna do the 'Cash for trash!' routine, right? So why don't we go outside the school district where they don't know us?"

"Yeh, that'd make yellin' 'Cash for trash!' a lot easier, huh?"

Pushing the large cart steadily, the group passed behind the shopping district to an industrial area with many small factories.

"Ms. Kotani, there's a lot of houses right behind there."

"Right. Let's try to work there."

They came upon a narrow back street, which was lined with modern apartments on both sides.

"This looks good, doesn't it, Jun?"

"Yeh," he answered. Then he made up his mind and started shouting. "Do ya have any trash? Newspaper! Magazines! Old clothes!"

A group of mothers cradling babies in their arms looked over at them. The odd combination must have surprised them, for they started whispering amongst themselves. Ms. Kotani was pretty and her skin was fair. On top of that, she had kids with her. No wonder they were curious.

Ms. Kotani couldn't help feeling self-conscious, and in spite of herself, she lowered her head. But that only made things worse, and the housewives started looking her over.

"Jun, let's go," she said, unable to stand it. Pulling the rattling cart behind her, she hotfooted it out of there at last.

"What're ya doin'!" complained Jun as he chased after her.

Ms. Kotani pulled out a handkerchief and wiped the sweat from her face. It was a cold sweat.

"I wish I were a dog like Lucky."

"What're ya talkin' about, Ms Kotani?" said Jun, encouraging her. "You can do it."

"You're embarrassed?" asked Misae, peeking up at Ms. Kotani's face. "How 'bout you, Tetsuzo? Are you embarrassed?"

Tetsuzo shook his head.

"Nobody's embarrassed but you, Ms. Kotani. Adults are so much trouble."

Ms. Kotani was disheartened, but rallying herself, she went down another side street.

"Jun, this time, don't call out. Let's just go house by house."

"Sure, that'd be okay."

They left the cart on the side of the street and started going door-to-door.

"Excuse me, do you have any newspaper or old magazines?" asked Ms. Kotani. She had managed to spit this out smoothly, which was a relief, but things went downhill from there.

"If you're collecting junk, go around to the back! Geez! Coming to the front door to get trash!"

Flustered, Ms. Kotani rushed away.

What a mistake! She had no idea that junk collectors were supposed to go to the back door. Teachers truly were ignorant. She broke into a cold sweat again.

"Excuse me!" called Ms. Kotani, knocking on another door.

A large man in pajamas answered.

"What'd ya want?"

"Do you have any old newspapers or magazines?"

"You're a trash collector?"

"Yes."

She wasn't really, but it would have been pointless to deny it.

"See those bottles under the floorboard? Take those."

Ms. Kotani could see that it was extremely dirty under the floor, but she couldn't very well turn him down now. She had no choice but to crawl in and pull the dirty things out. In an instant, her pretty face was all smudged with dirt. She went to pay the man some money, but he waved her away.

"No, that's okay," he said. "You can have 'em. A young thing like you shouldn't be doing such worthless work anyway. Can't you find anything better?"

She wanted to tell him to leave her the hell alone, but she couldn't.

"I'm not a beggar," she said instead, "so I'll leave the money here."

She hurried off immediately, but she was boiling with rage. You big fat bear! Blockhead! Nitwit! Ignoramus! Fool! Idiot! One foul term of abuse after another popped into her head. Now she could understand why the disposal plant children used bad language.

Jun and Misae did the rounds, and even Tetsuzo got in on the act.

"Ma'am," Misae would ask, very politely. "Do ya have any old newspapers or magazines?"

Tetsuzo would just yank open the door, stick in his head, and curtly say, "Newspaper."

"What do you mean, 'newspaper'?"

When the person came to the door to see what he wanted, Tetsuzo merely pointed to the cart in silence.

Ms. Kotani could see that just one word was enough to get the message across. Tetsuzo was doing it his way.

Their strenuous efforts, however, were in vain, and their harvest was woefully inadequate. Apparently, even junk collectors had their own territory, and people were reluctant to give anything to strangers. All four of them were exhausted and discouraged.

They came upon a vacant lot with a large sewage pipe. Ms. Kotani went and bought some Popsicles, and when she returned, she plopped down on top of the pipe.

"Let's take a break."

She was so thirsty that the Popsicle tasted extremely delicious, but it did little to revive her spirits.

"We still don't got much," Jun moaned pathetically. "I wonder how Tokuji and the others are doin'."

"Collectin' trash is a lot harder than we thought, isn't it?" said Misae.

"It sure is."

Ms. Kotani smiled and stroked Misae's hair. Misae was exactly right. Sure, junk collectors just had to collect newspaper, magazines, bottles, and other stuff, but they also had to contend with the embarrassment and even humiliation of the work. Every trade had its difficulties. People who made fun of junk collectors should have to try it for a while. Maybe then they would change their attitudes. Ms. Kotani wanted to put that big bear man to work first.

Suddenly, something came lumbering out of the drainage pipe, and Ms. Kotani jumped up and screamed. Jun stood up to shield her.

"Hello there, young man, and a good afternoon," said the queer man that emerged from the pipe. His hair hung down to his shoulders, and his face peeked from behind a bushy beard. His clothes, which were covered with gaudy patches, were an odd mix of Western and Japanese styles. Depending on how you looked at it, the design had a certain flair of its own.

"Are you a beggar?" asked Misae, unconcernedly.

"I was a beggar in the past, young lady, but as thou may observe, I have abandoned that profession," said the queer man, spreading out his arms like a Shakespearean actor.

Misae was thrilled and sat down in front of him.

"Young lady, will thou not offer alms to me? Thou hast half

of thy Popsicle remaining. When the wealthy offer alms to the poor, they become justified in the eyes of God. *Bakushi*!"

"What's that, mister? What's '*bakushi*'?"

"Excellent question! I thank thee for listening so closely. '*Bakushi*' is an Indian word, and it means that in the loving spirit of God, and in the loving spirit of a nice young lady, to share that . . ."

"What? It just means ya want my Popsicle!"

"What a sagacious and wise young lady!" said the man, spreading his arms dramatically as before.

"You're weird," said Misae, handing over her half-eaten Popsicle. The man gave Ms. Kotani the creeps.

"And what an attractive young woman we have here!" he said, indicating Ms. Kotani. "I may soon be blinded by her dazzling beauty!"

Maybe he wasn't so bad after all. Jun sat down again, and Ms. Kotani squatted on the ground. But she didn't feel relaxed.

"So what might thou relation be? Don't tell me thou art a mother and her children."

"No. She's a teacher. And we're students," said Jun, still sucking on his Popsicle.

"What a surprise! And why would a teacher be working as a junk collector?"

Jun acted put out, but he gave a brief explanation of their situation.

"What a shockingly beautiful tale! I, a humble samurai, am

deeply and painfully moved. I must commend thee from the bottom of my heart."

"Hey, mister, ya talk like you're in an old play or something," said Misae.

"A humble samurai despises the present age. I disdain electricity, automobiles, and all vestiges of the modern era. I do, however, like Popsicles."

Misae giggled.

"Well, then, leave it to thy humble samurai," said the queer man, standing up. Pulling the cart by himself, he strode off gallantly. Jun and the others chased after him.

"Jun, I wonder if it's okay."

"He doesn't seem bad."

"I'm not saying he is."

The man entered the same side street that Ms. Kotani had ignobly run out of earlier. He parked the cart in the middle of the street and started chattering away in a loud voice.

"The humble samurai has arrived! Bring out thy trash! Bring out thy trash! The humble samurai has arrived!"

At the sound of his voice, children came running from every direction.

"It's the Humble Samurai!" they yelled. He obviously was quite popular.

"Hear ye! Hear ye! All who have gathered from near and far! Today, I have come not for myself. No! Today, thou art to witness the one good deed of this humble samurai's life. Here with me today is the Princess Teacher, a person of high lineage and noble birth. She has concealed herself for the time being as a humble junk collector, and in her mercy, the great mercy of a goddess of mercy, she has worked day after day, night after night, to raise the funds to pay for the hospital bill of one of her students, who has polio."

"Hey, mister, I never said that," complained Jun, as he stared at the man in disbelief.

"Leave it to me, son, leave it to me," the man answered, completely unconcerned.

"In this day and age," he continued, "when one encounters a beautiful story, one wants to share it with others. Even the monks at the 'Purification of the Self' Temple of Rokuharamitsuji should reflect on this humble, yet beautiful narrative. So, come on, bring out thy stuff."

Ms. Kotani was totally taken aback. Geez! He was just spitting out whatever popped into his head! In his brazenness, he resembled Mr. Adachi.

In an instant, they had collected various waste articles, and their group had to get to work. Ms. Kotani ran around frantically trying to get everything weighed.

The man headed into another side street and started yelling the same sorts of things. Within an hour, their cart was piled to the limit.

"Thank you very much," said Ms. Kotani appreciatively, "this is all that we can carry."

"Thank you, Mr. Humble Samurai," said Misae.

"We appreciate it," said Jun.

"Mister, we're kids from the disposal plant across the way. Come and see us some time."

"I would be most honored," said the peculiar man, abruptly turning back.

"Thank you, mister!"

"Hope to see you again!"

"Fare thee well!" said the man, sustaining his affected manner to the end.

That day, their group's cart was the undisputed winner. Mr. Adachi, Mr. Orihashi, and Mr. Ota gazed with wide-eyed disbelief, and Jun couldn't constrain his excitement.

21. My Heart Tingled

Ms. Kotani wrote "WHAT?" on the blackboard and turned to the class.

"This is the subject of today's writing lesson," she said.

"What the heck're ya talkin' about?" called out Katsuichi.

"You don't know what the heck I'm talking about. That's why today's topic is 'What?'" She said this with a straight face, which made everyone laugh.

Many of the teachers at the back of the room laughed, too. This was Ms. Kotani's first time to be observed, so she was extremely nervous and uptight. She just couldn't be laid back like Mr. Adachi.

"At the top of your paper, please write 'What?' After that, please write, 'Ms. Kotani came into class carrying a large package.' Everyone's first sentence will be the same, but after that, you can write whatever you want. Just write what you think."

After she finished her explanation, she stepped out into the hallway. A moment later, she returned carrying a heavy-looking package. It was about three feet square and wrapped in a white cloth.

"Wow! It's huge!" the students called out in unison.

"It's big, isn't it?" said Ms. Kotani. "But what is it?"

"A TV!" yelled Katsuichi.

"A stove!"

"A fan!"

One after another, the students yelled out their ideas.

"Well, then, write down exactly what you think. And it'll be a better composition if you write down your reasons, too."

Nearly every head dropped down to write. Only Tetsuzo kept staring at the box.

"Okay, Junichi, could you read what you wrote? From the beginning, please."

Junichi stood up and read.

"'Ms. Kotani came into class carrying a large package. I wondered what it was. Everybody yelled things like "a TV" or "a stove." I thought maybe it was a TV, but if you guess too soon and get it wrong, you end up losing, so I decided just to write that I don't know.'"

Some of the teachers at the back of the room smiled unconsciously. Junichi's composition was very much in character.

"Now, I'm going to unwrap it," said Ms. Kotani. She removed the white cloth and revealed the cardboard box of a television.

"A TV! Just like I said!" burst out Katsuichi with joy.

"Okay, please continue writing."

Ms. Kotani waited until they were finished.

"Okay, Katsuichi. Just read the new part."

"'It was a TV, just as I thought. I guessed right on the first try. I'm pretty proud of myself, and I toot my horn.'"

Junichi seemed doubtful, and Tetsuzo continued staring.

"Okay, let's see what's next."

Ms. Kotani tore open the cardboard box and pulled out a

smaller box, which had a picture of a tangerine on the side. The students started screaming and yelling, and the teachers at the back laughed.

The students' pens started moving again.

"It doesn't seem to be a TV, so let's see what Katsuichi wrote. Okay, Katsuichi, pick up where you left off."

Katsuichi stood up and read.

"'Ms. Kotani's unfair. She tricked me.'"

The teachers burst out laughing, and Mr. Orihashi laughed so hard that tears came to his eyes.

"Sorry about that, Katsuichi. Maybe you'll guess right next time."

She went over to where he was sitting and patted him on the head.

"Look what's inside," she said, tearing off the lid and tilting the box for the students to see.

It was packed with crumpled up balls of newspaper or perhaps tangerines wrapped up in individual sheets.

"Don't let her trick you, you guys!" called out Junichi.

"That's right. Don't let me trick you. Give it some thought, and write down what you think."

Mr. Adachi, who was watching from the back, was impressed. Every student was engaged, and not one of them was looking out the window or daydreaming. Her class had really changed.

"Michiko, could we hear from you next, please?"

"Okay. 'I think they're apples because there are round things wrapped in newspaper. I don't think they're tangerines because I looked in Ms. Kotani's eyes and could tell that she was lying.'"

Ms. Kotani removed the balls of newspaper and showed the class that they were empty. Then she reached into the box and pulled out four cake boxes. The students started screaming and yelling again.

"Is it cake, Ms. Kotani?"

"I have no idea," she answered.

"Do they all have the same thing in them?" asked Terue.

"Yes, they do. But I guess it's mean to only let you look. I've reconsidered and have decided to let you hear it, too. Now listen closely to what kind of sound it makes. Okay?"

She shook the box, and it made a rustling noise. The other three boxes made the same sound.

"Now I know," said Takeshi.

"I know!"

"I know!"

Voices called out from all over the classroom.

"Can you really be so sure?" Ms. Kotani asked.

"Yeh, it's absolutely gotta be," said Takeshi, sounding cocky.

"Well, then, write it down."

Some students were already writing. Ms. Kotani had come up with a great class. If she kept going like this, the students would have long compositions before they knew it. And since they were constantly keyed up, they were bound to write interesting sentences.

"Okay, Takeshi, read yours, please."

"'Ms. Kotani has gone to a lot of trouble trying to trick us. But since she let us hear how it sounds, I knew right away what it was. I could hear the fireworks going off in my head. It's candy wrapped in paper. That sound was a clear giveaway. She's going to give us some candy to apologize for tricking us. I knew she was all right. Hurray for Ms. Kotani!'"

The teachers at the back laughed again, and so did Ms. Kotani.

"So you think you know, huh? You think it's candy, right?"

"Isn't it?" asked Takeshi, looking worried.

"I don't know. What do you think?"

"It's candy, isn't it?"

"It's definitely candy!"

Ms. Kotani was in danger of being lynched if she didn't cough up some candy.

"Okay, I'll let you hold the box to see if there's any candy in it."

She passed one box to each of the four groups, and the students started shaking and smelling them.

"There's something in it!" burst out one of the students.

"You idiot! We knew that from the beginning!" said Takeshi. But Hiromichi, the boy who yelled, apparently meant something else.

"Listen! You can hear something scurryin' around inside."

"He's right!" others yelled in surprise. No one had noticed

because they started shaking the box as soon as they got it in their hands.

"It's a turtle!" someone called out.

"It's gotta be a turtle!"

Turtles would be better than candy. The students were ecstatic, and they kept their eyes on their boxes as they wrote. When they heard something hard banging against the sides, they could barely concentrate. Tetsuzo's gaze was riveted to his box from the moment he learned there was a living thing inside it.

"Hiromichi, could you read yours, please?"

"'It's a turtle. It's gotta be. I prayed to God about it and asked that it be a turtle. Ms. Kotani, please let me have one.'"

"Oh, brother! What am I going to do with you guys?" she said. "Just before, you said it absolutely had to be candy. Maybe you're wrong this time, too."

The students looked worried.

"But it's not any fun teasing you like this, so why don't I just tell you what's inside?"

The students shouted for joy.

"So what are you feeling right now?" asked Ms. Kotani.

"My heart's beating like crazy."

"I'm gonna faint."

"I gotta go to the bathroom."

The students yelled out all kinds of stuff.

"I want you to remember how you feel right now, okay?"

She went around and slit the seals with her utility knife.

"Okay, everybody, on the count of three, you can open the boxes. Ready? One . . . two . . . three."

The giddy students opened their treasures, and a shout of joy went up as the sight of lively red crayfish leapt out at them.

Ms. Kotani let them scream and yell for a while.

"There's one for each of you, so do a good job taking care of them."

"Yippeee!" yelled Takeshi, at the top of his lungs.

Ms. Kotani wouldn't be getting lynched after all.

"Okay, look at me, please," she said. "Keep up the good work for just a little bit more. Up until now, the most exciting moments were just before you opened the boxes and just after you found out what was inside. For the final part of your compositions, I want you to write exactly how you felt at those two moments."

"Okaaay!" the students answered cheerfully, turning back to their work.

The teachers at the back of the room were extremely impressed. First-graders had a tough time writing even simple compositions, so it was difficult to imagine an entire class picking up their pencils just because their teacher told them to start writing.

The shelves at the back of the room were lined with the students' diaries. Each and every one was worn out from frequent use, which spoke volumes about how much Ms. Kotani and her class had struggled.

Mr. Ota had arrived early and spent some time skimming through them. He was especially struck by something that he read in the diary of a boy named Satoru. Satoru's diary revealed the secret of why the students in Ms. Kotani's class wrote so fluently.

"We started our diarys about the midle of the second samester. Every morning we gotta get up early and go to school and show Ms Kotani what we wrot. Its kinda hard geting up early. I never got time to play any more. I wrot a little bit, but then I ran out of stuf to say. Ms Kotani told me to try harder. The next day I wrot two more lines than before, and then I wrot that I was dun and that I realy hate diarys. Then Ms Kotani wrot me this note.

> Dear Satoru,
> It was good that you were honest about hating diaries. But if you have really struggled, you are sure to look back at this time and be happy that you went to the trouble. It's good to struggle sometimes. Push yourself to be as fine and bright as you can. Writing is painful. When I finish writing at night, my teeth start to rattle, and it hurts when I try to eat. Do your teeth hurt when you're finished writing? I bet they don't. I'm sure you can try harder.

When I dont got stuf to write about, I go off and explor. If you go to diferent places, then you fine stuf to write about. When

I just feel like being laizy, I remember what Ms Kotani wrot to me, and then I can try harder."

Ms. Kotani was rather nervous. Tetsuzo had picked up his pencil and was writing something. She casually wandered over to his desk and saw that he was writing away with determination. Her heart skipped a beat.

After assuring herself that Tetsuzo was done writing, she asked the class if everyone was finished.

"Yes!" called out the students.

"Whose should I read this time?"

Ms. Kotani didn't know what to do. This was the first time that Tetsuzo had ever written anything, and she very much wanted to read it before the class. But if it didn't make any sense, she would only humiliate him. What should she do? Her head was swimming, but a voice told her that she should believe in her students. She decided to trust him.

"Let's read Tetsuzo's," she said, picking up his paper. She skimmed it over and prayed that it was all right.

i wuz starin an starin an than i wuz starin and starin al the wae in side the boks a red gi cam ote mi noz tingld lik wen u drnk sodu pop an mi hart tingld two i luv red gies and i luv mz kotani

Ms. Kotani read in a loud voice, "'I was staring and staring. And then I was staring and staring all the way inside the box. A red guy came out. My nose tingled like when you drink soda pop, and my heart tingled, too. I love red guys. And I love Ms. Kotani.'"

Ms. Kotani's voice began to quiver when she reached the part about Tetsuzo loving her, and her eyes filled with tears. She couldn't control herself, and she turned away. One student started clapping, and then another, and gradually, the applause built to a crescendo. Mr. Adachi was clapping. Mr. Orihashi was clapping. Everyone was clapping.

The wave of applause shook the classroom.

22. Ripples

Tetsuzo was absent, which worried Ms. Kotani. Up to then, he had never missed a day of school. During recess, she casually mentioned her concern to Mr. Adachi.

"Really?" he said, with surprise. "Misae's absent, too."

When Mr. Orihashi mentioned that Keiko hadn't shown up either, they hurriedly checked on the attendance of the other disposal plant children.

Thrown into a panic, the Assistant Principal rushed off to the principal's office. A few minutes later, Mr. Adachi was called in.

"Mr. Adachi," said the Principal, "all of the students from the disposal plant are absent."

"Yes, apparently so."

"Do you think it's a student strike?"

Mr. Adachi scratched his head. Even he didn't know. Would the disposal plant parents have their children stay home without even contacting the school? They hadn't even sent word to Mr. Adachi or other teachers that they trusted, so he couldn't understand it.

"Just the same, I'd like you to go out there and see what's going on."

The Assistant Principal offered to go, too, but the Principal answered that he preferred that Mr. Adachi go alone, in order to avoid aggravating the situation.

An hour later, Mr. Adachi still hadn't returned. The Principal couldn't suppress his irritation and paced back and forth in his office. Ms. Kotani and Mr. Orihashi rushed to the teachers' room as soon as their classes were over, and when they heard that there was still no word, they turned back to their classrooms with anxious expressions.

Mr. Ota's next period was Arts and Crafts, which was being taught by a special teacher.

"If I hear anything," he told Ms. Kotani and Mr. Orihashi, "I'll go to your rooms and tell you. So just relax and teach your classes."

It was nearly noon by the time Mr. Adachi returned.

"So how did it go?" the Principal asked impatiently.

"It's pretty bad," Mr. Adachi answered bluntly. He was in a horrible mood. "Yesterday, there was supposed to be a meeting at the disposal plant to explain about the relocation plan, but the city only sent two lousy officials, both of them extremely young. Well, to get right to the point, the parents at the disposal plant are furious about two things. The first is that the decision was made suddenly and unilaterally. Even though the city employees at the plant were given a detailed explanation a full month ago, the temporary employees were merely notified that they would have to relocate. The second thing they're mad about is that when Tokuji's father asked about the children's school situation, he was told that they'd just have to go to the school they were assigned to. In other words, they're all being ordered to transfer. Isao's father explained that the roads through the landfill are in bad shape, and that with all the dump trucks, it would be really dangerous for kids. What do you think those guys said to that?"

"I'd like to hear," said the Principal, leaning forward.

Mr. Adachi couldn't hide his disgust.

"Nowadays even dogs avoid cars. Did you get that? They actually said that nowadays even dogs avoid cars!"

"What a stupid and nasty thing to say," said the Principal, making a sour face.

After that, the Principal and the Assistant Principal spent another hour discussing the situation in detail with Mr. Adachi.

It was Wednesday, so Ms. Kotani didn't have any classes in the afternoon. Mr. Orihashi was also free because his students had special classes, so they decided to go to the disposal plant together to see what was going on.

The children were gathered at their fort, with their books and study materials scattered all over the place. Apparently, they were playing school. When the two teachers showed up, the children shouted for joy and came running over.

"Adachi was just here, ya know."

"Yeh, we know," said Mr. Orihashi.

"How commendable! So you're studying together, huh?" said Ms. Kotani.

"Me, Jun, and Shigeko are the teachers," bragged Isao.

"Do ya know what my brother does, Ms. Kotani?" complained Misae. "If we don't know the answer to a question, he hits us with the rubber hose. Tetsuzo got hit once, too."

"I've been hit three times!" said Koji.

"These guys are slow learners, Ms. Kotani," explained Jun, who was beginning to get cold feet.

When Ms. Kotani pictured Tetsuzo being thrown for a loop simply because he was asked to add five to eight, she couldn't help but smile. She couldn't imagine how he would have reacted to being hit with a hose.

"Even so, I can't believe you guys went on strike," said Mr. Orihashi. "That's pretty cool."

"What's cool about it?" Isao snapped back at him. "I gotta teach all the squirts, and since we got so much time, it's really boring. I don't get anything out of this. I wanna go back to school."

"I guess you're right. Sorry about that," said Mr. Orihashi, apologizing for his insensitive remark.

"At first, we fought with our parents about it and asked 'em why we gotta stay home from school."

Mr. Orihashi flinched at the thought of these children turning on their parents en masse.

"But we don't wanna be sold down the river any more than they do."

Ms. Kotani wasn't sure who first used this phrase, but it certainly was a clever way of putting it. What was happening to the disposal plant residents was a present-day example of being sold down the river.

"And we'd never get to see you guys again," said Jun, dejectedly.

"That's why we're doin' the best we can."

"Okay, okay. I'm sorry," said Mr. Orihashi. "I shouldn't have said that." He was a large man, but he was beginning to feel rather small.

When they returned from the disposal plant, Mr. Orihashi immediately went to the principal's office.

"It's just my idea," he said to the Principal, "but if the students from the disposal plant aren't going to come to school, I think some teachers should have to go out there and do some classes. It's a crime for us to just stand by and do nothing while students are missing classes. Don't you agree?"

"I think your enthusiasm is just fine," said the Principal, "but I don't like your suggestion that we're standing by doing nothing. I'm doing everything in my power, and in spite of what you might think, I'm going to a lot of trouble to solve this problem."

"Sorry about that. I apologize if I went too far. But could you at least consider my idea of having teachers go out there?"

"Hmm," said the Principal, musing over the idea.

At about three o'clock, the Principal called the head teachers for each grade level and the homeroom teachers with students from the disposal plant into his office, and they considered Mr. Orihashi's proposal. It was decided that teachers couldn't be forced to take on extra duties, but that anyone who wanted to do the classes would be allowed to. Mr. Orihashi was extremely dissatisfied.

In the end, only four teachers went to the disposal plant that day. Ms. Kotani recalled her first visit to the disposal plant when Shiro had shocked her with a bitter accusation.

"Most of 'em just make fools of us," he had said. "They say we stink and that we're stupid. They don't even treat us like human beings!"

As much as Ms. Kotani hated to admit it, Shiro had spoken the truth. He had also said that Adachi, Orihashi, and Ota were the only good teachers at Himematsu Elementary School. The children at the plant had seen through their teachers long ago.

Three days after the students started their strike, something ironic happened. A large headline, reporting on Tetsuzo's fly research, appeared in the newspaper:

Six-Year-Old Fly Professor Solves Health Department's Problem

Along with a picture of Tetsuzo gazing at his bottles and taking records, the article reported on how he helped the ham factory get rid of their flies. It also reported on his research on various aspects of fly ecology, and on his current research, which was whether flies had preferences for certain colors. The article was extremely detailed.

Another large headline in the local news section read:

Students Strike in Protest of Disposal Plant Transfer

People reading the headlines would never have imagined that they concerned the same person. When the Principal saw the articles, he nearly pulled his hair out. It was the first time that his school had appeared twice in the same paper. Mr. Adachi, on the other hand, laughed and slapped his knee. Needless to say, he was happy about the article on Tetsuzo, but he also seemed to feel that the disposal plant incident should be made public in order to bring injustice to light. Ms. Kotani gazed and gazed at Tetsuzo's picture, the memories undoubtedly flooding her all at once.

The disposal plant children scrambled to get a copy of the newspaper so they could read the articles. Isao read them for Tetsuzo and Misae, and Jun explained all the difficult words.

"Tetsuzo, it's all about you! Aren't you even gonna crack a smile?"

"Ah," answered Tetsuzo, who was practicing his writing with his butt sticking up in the air.

"You really are unfriendly," said Shiro, looking disgusted.

Shortly after the incident appeared in the newspaper, officials from City Hall came to the disposal plant for the first time. This time, the head of the department attended. The four teachers who were teaching the disposal plant children, the Principal, and the Assistant Principal represented the school.

"To begin with, I would like to express my deep appreciation for all the hard work you've put in over the years," began the department head, bowing deeply.

The parents from the disposal plant bowed politely in return.

"Now, then," he continued, "I would like to humbly apologize for our having incurred your displeasure through our inept handling of the situation. I heard from the men that visited you the other day about your discontent, and I must say that all of your points are quite reasonable. We delayed explaining the situation only because we were anxious about upsetting you. I want to assure you that we had no intention whatsoever of discriminating against you. As for the problem about the children commuting to school, as you all know, the school districts are determined ahead of time, and it is completely out of our power to do anything about that. It's natural that you would be concerned about traffic accidents, and we have contacted the relevant authorities about the matter. We will do whatever is in our power to solve this problem. In exchange, I would like to ask you to be cooperative in dealing with the plant relocation."

Again, the department head bowed.

"Pretty polite talk from somebody who's screwing us," said Mr. Adachi, in a voice the department head could hear.

Tokuji's father stood up and condemned the young men from the other day for their rude comments. The department head whispered something to the man sitting next to him, and the man stood up.

"That's the first we've heard about that," he said, "and we

apologize. But they're young, and I'm sure they just made a slip of the tongue."

"What's that supposed to mean?" asked Tokuji's father. "That only suggests that they mistakenly revealed your true attitude."

"No, I certainly don't mean to suggest that . . ."

"Do you have children?"

"Yes, I do."

"And how would you feel if he said that about *your* children?"

"I'd feel the same way you do. I'd be angry."

"But he would never say something like that to you, would he? To us, he's willing to say something that anyone would find insulting, but to you, a person in authority, he would never even think about it. That sounds like discrimination to me."

"Excuse me!" said Mr. Baku, raising his hand. "You should know that before we decided to have our children stay home from school, everybody was talking about going on strike. Nobody wants to do this kind of dirty work nowadays, and if we went on strike, you'd immediately have a major problem on your hands. But you know what? I told everyone that we shouldn't do what other people would do, and that we shouldn't rejoice in doing something that would cause other people trouble. We should see our work through to the end, no matter how tough it might be. That's the way to resist. But let me tell you, mister, everybody's got their breaking point. And workers got the right to go on strike. Like Mr. Adachi said, only your way of talking is polite. I don't think you have any intention of really listening to how we feel."

Mr. Baku spoke slowly and looked the department head straight in the eye.

"Mister, did you see this newspaper? Well, the six-year-old Fly Professor here is actually my grandson. When he first entered this school, he was like a stone. He never talked. He never wrote anything. He never opened his books. If he really were a stone, he would never cause any harm, but when he gets upset about something, he scratches and bites whatever's in his path. You see that attractive, young teacher over there? Well, she's been scratched, and she's shed quite a few tears, but she's struggled more than words can say, and she's brought my grandson to the point that he's now known as the Fly Professor. That's the sacred beauty that you're casually ripping up with your foregone decision and easily spoken words. What we're saying is that we can't permit that."

Chills ran down Ms. Kotani's spine. Mr. Baku spoke in a quiet, gentle tone of voice, but his words were harsh.

"My grandson and I live alone, and we don't have any relatives. Everyone that works at the disposal plant is burdened with a pretty difficult life. We don't need your sympathy. We're ordinary people making an ordinary appeal. You need only to listen in an ordinary way."

Just then, a young man was brought forward.

"Mr. Shirai," said the department head in a theatrically stern tone of voice. "I want you to apologize for your inappropriate comments of the other day."

"I am very sorry," said Mr. Shirai, without the slightest resistance. "I sincerely apologize for what I said." It was as if it had been staged ahead of time.

"They just don't get it, do they?" lamented Mr. Baku, shaking his head in disbelief.

23. Tetsuzo's Not Bad

Ms. Kotani was erasing the blackboard at the end of the second period when Michiko came up to her.

"Ms. Kotani," she asked. "Why doesn't Tetsuzo come to school anymore?"

Ms. Kotani had been dreading this question and wasn't sure how to answer it. Just then, Katsuichi came over and answered for her.

"Tetsuzo went on strike, didn't he, Ms. Kotani?"

"What's a 'strike'?" asked Michiko.

"It means to be absent."

"I know he's absent. But I wanna know *why* he's absent?"

"It's 'cause he might have to change schools. Right, Ms. Kotani?"

Katsuichi's parents had obviously kept him informed.

"Why are they makin' him change schools?"

By this point in the conversation, throngs of students had gathered around to hear what their teacher would say.

"Yeh, Ms. Kotani. Tetsuzo hasn't done anything wrong, so why are they making him change schools?"

"There are lots of reasons, and it's kind of complicated, but the disposal plant where he lives has to move. If one of you moved, you'd have to change schools, right? The problem, though, is that the people living at the disposal plant don't want to move. They're being forced to move for the convenience of the bureaucrats down at City Hall. But what's convenient for the bureaucrats is also convenient for the people living around here, so it's a big problem."

The students only seemed to partially understand what she was saying.

"It's bad for the school that ash is always falling, right?" said Michiko.

"That's right."

"I don't get it," said Michiko, tilting her head in confusion. "Wouldn't it be best just to move the disposal plant, and let Tetsuzo and the others live near here like us? My dad takes the train to work, so what's the problem?"

Ms. Kotani couldn't understand it either. Why couldn't the bureaucrats even consider what a first-grader could see was an obvious solution?

"Yeh, especially since he's only been doin' good stuff lately," muttered Takeshi, who must have been standing there for a while. "Just the other day, my mom was saying how hard it is to get in the newspaper. She said I should do something good enough to get in the paper, too."

"I wouldn't say something was good, just because it got into the newspaper," laughed Ms. Kotani. "But Tetsuzo hasn't done anything wrong, so it's really sad that he can't come to school. It's really painful for me, too."

"Minako's gone, and now Tetsuzo. You must really miss them, huh?" murmured Junichi, who was standing towards the back of the group.

The affair gradually became a major issue. The Board of Education sent an evaluation team, the Teachers Union got involved, and the PTA began holding frequent meetings. Even so, Ms. Kotani's anxiety intensified. She was pleased that so many people came to investigate, but she wondered whether they would truly understand the feelings of the disposal plant people and their children.

A teachers' meeting was held at the school. Most of the teachers sympathized with the disposal plant children, but they felt that holding a strike was going too far, and that it was wrong of the parents to let their children get mixed up in the dispute. At the PTA meetings, many of the parents took a similar position.

Ms. Kotani despaired of the many teachers and parents who paid lip service to what was right or wrong, while doing absolutely nothing. Mr. Baku's words came to mind.

"If we went on strike," he had said, "you'd immediately have a major problem on your hands. But I told everyone that we shouldn't do what other people would do, and that we shouldn't rejoice in doing something that would cause other people trouble. We should see our work through to the end, no matter how tough it might be. That's the way to resist."

Ms. Kotani wanted to live as Mr. Baku did. She went to Mr. Adachi for advice.

"Why don't we pass out fliers in front of the station?" she asked him. "I feel like I'm doing the kids a disservice by being so complacent. I don't think doing the special classes is enough."

Mr. Adachi was highly in favor of the idea. He said he was getting frustrated with teachers that were totally unresponsive, no matter how often they spoke about the problem at the teachers' meetings.

Mr. Adachi handled the wording of the flier, in consultation with the people at the disposal plant.

A Plea to the Public

As you know from recent articles in the newspaper, it has been decided that the town's garbage disposal plant will be relocated to the number three landfill. The current disposal plant was built fifty-five years ago and has not received any major repairs since. The method of trash disposal is so extremely primitive that ash rains down on the homes in the area.

Relocating an antiquated plant in the middle of a residential area to a landfill with modern facilities is a good idea. We are highly in favor of the relocation. The newspaper reports have given the impression that we are opposed to the relocation itself, but that is not at all the case.

We have worked hard, in horrible conditions, without grumble or complaint. We live inside the disposal plant compound because housing was promised to us when we were hired. During the summer, there is the stench of rotting trash. During the winter, there is falling ash. But we have never complained.

Now, with the relocation of the plant, it has been decided that we have to live in prefabricated housing that has been set up next to the new plant. From this location, however, it will take fifty minutes to make a roundtrip to the nearest market, and forty minutes for our children to walk to school. As you know, there are many construction vehicles going through the landfill, and the roads have not been improved. It is reprehensible to force children to live in such an area.

We are making the following demands, and as human beings, we should be able to expect at least this much.

The permanent hiring of all disposal plant workers, and an end to temporary employment.

Construction of housing at the old plant, with tenancy priority given to plant workers.

We are counting on an outpouring of public support.

Trash Disposal Plant Workers
Concerned Teachers of Himematsu
Elementary School

The small group of teachers gained another supporter. Ms. Yoko Egawa, the Arts and Crafts teacher, said that if they were going to distribute fliers, she wanted to help. She was a young teacher, so Ms. Kotani felt rather encouraged.

The five teachers agreed to come to school half an hour early, which was when Ms. Kotani usually did the "morning diary." She explained the situation to the class and asked them to let her miss a few days.

"It's okay, Ms. Kotani, we'll just go ahead and keep writin', and you can read 'em when Tetsuzo comes back."

After dividing up the work, the teachers and plant workers headed off to train stations, bus stops, and other busy locations. Ms. Kotani was paired with Ms. Egawa, who seemed a bit uncomfortable about doing such work. Ms. Kotani had gotten used to collecting trash, so handing out fliers didn't seem like such a big deal.

About five minutes after they started, Jun, Misae, and Tetsuzo came running up. Their faces were flushed and they were panting heavily.

"We're gonna pass out fliers out, too, Ms. Kotani," said Misae.

"Everybody discussed it, and we decided to help," Jun explained.

Ms. Kotani was hesitant. Was it a good idea to let children distribute fliers? Even if she said no, they were already being criticized from various quarters for using the children as pawns in a dispute.

"It's really about us, isn't it?" prodded Jun.

That clinched it for her, and she handed him some fliers.

People started pouring out of the train station, and the small group was soon scrambling like madmen to keep up.

"Boy, we really gotta hustle!" cried Jun.

Initially, Misae asked each person to please read the flyer, but before long, she was saying, "Here, here," and pressing them against their chests. The latter method proved much more efficient.

"Oh, I almost forgot," said Jun. "Hey, Tetsutsun! Come here!"

Jun unfastened his belt and pulled out two large pieces of construction paper fastened together with rubber bands. He draped the papers over Tetsuzo's head and turned him into a walking billboard. In rather poor handwriting was written, "I'm the famous Fly Professor! Help me continue my research!"

"Whose idea was this?" asked Ms. Kotani.

"Mine!" boasted Jun.

"No way. This is going too far."

"But everything's advertising these days, Ms. Kotani!"

"No way. This time you lose. Besides, I don't think it's so much your idea. You're just copying adults."

"If you put it that way, I guess you're right."

Jun was disappointed, but Ms. Kotani yanked the papers off Tetsuzo immediately.

"It's the Humble Samurai!" yelled Misae. "Hey! Humble Samurai!"

The strange man was pushing a handmade cart on the opposite side of the railroad tracks. Apparently hearing Misae's yell, he turned in their direction and raised his hand in a friendly greeting. Then he started heading towards them.

"Who's that?" asked Ms. Egawa.

"It's hard to explain," said Ms. Kotani, not knowing how to answer.

"Well, hello, there," said the Humble Samurai. "And what might thou be trading in today?"

Ms. Kotani felt a bit self-conscious about always being seen by him in awkward situations, but she properly expressed her appreciation just the same.

"Thank you for the other day," she said.

"We're on strike, mister," said Misae.

"On strike?" asked the Humble Samurai, gaping at them. "Thou art not attending thy school?"

"That's right, we're on strike."

"And thy teachers hast joined thee?"

Ms. Kotani didn't know what to say. Things always got weird when this guy was around.

"Jun, you explain it to him," she said.

The Humble Samurai listened intently to Jun's explanation and read over the flier. That seemed to satisfy him.

"Very well, then," he said, pounding his chest, "leave it to thy humble samurai."

Ms. Kotani dreaded what he might yell this time.

Suddenly, he started dancing to his own sonorous rendition of *Kuroda-bushi*, a lively old song sometimes sung at weddings. Ms. Egawa turned red. A crowd started to form, and as the spectators gazed amusedly at the spectacle, Jun and the others passed out their fliers.

They certainly could have managed without the man's help, but Ms. Kotani was pleased to have received his goodwill. For a young female teacher like Ms. Egawa, however, the shock might have been too intense.

At three o'clock in the afternoon, Tetsuzo was home alone. He took down the clay figurine that he had received from Ms. Kotani and started practicing his sketching.

"Tetsuzo!" someone called out.

Standing in the doorway were Takeshi, Katsuichi, Bunji, and about five other children.

Tetsuzo was confused. Apart from the disposal plant children, he had never once had a friend come to play, and he didn't know how to act.

"Can we come in?" asked Takeshi.

"Ah," answered Tetsuzo.

"Tetsuzo, I'm sorry about takin' your flies that time," said Bunji.

"Ah," replied Tetsuzo, forgiving him.

"Tetsuzo, when're ya comin' back to school? Everybody's worried about you."

"Ah."

"This is a present from Michiko," said Takeshi, handing Tetsuzo a handkerchief covered with pictures of horseflies. Tetsuzo stared at the gift uncertainly, not knowing what to make of it.

"Wow, Tetsuzo, you're really good at drawin' flies," said Katsuichi, obviously impressed with the pictures on the walls. "Cool . . . impressive . . . incredible . . ." he muttered to himself as he walked around the room. "What's this one called?" he asked when he came across a rather unusual-looking fly.

"It's a female scuttle fly."

"But there's no wings."

"They don't got wings."

For the first time in his life, Tetsuzo had spoken with a friend. But to Katsuichi, Takeshi, and the others, nothing special had happened. If Ms. Kotani had been watching, she would have marveled at the mysterious nature of children.

Tetsuzo and his new friends played mountain breakdown, a game where you try to pull *shogi* pieces out of a pile without letting them click against the board.

Before long, Mr. Baku returned home from work. Standing transfixed in the doorway, he gazed at the spectacle of Tetsuzo playing with his friends, and quietly, he wiped away a tear.

24. Difficult Times

Exactly one week after the children started their school strike, two general meetings were held. One was a special general meeting of the Himematsu Elementary School PTA, which began precisely at two o'clock in the afternoon.

First, a chairman for the assembly was elected, and after he rattled off the customary words of acceptance and humility, he moved on to the issue at hand.

"As has been proposed," he began, "today's PTA meeting will deal with only one issue: to determine our public stance towards the trash disposal plant relocation. I am hoping for a thorough consideration of the issue. Today's meeting is not just another PTA meeting. As something of a town meeting, our public statement on this issue will have a serious impact on how the issue is resolved. We have invited all parties considered necessary to today's discussion, and we hope that all doubts on this issue will be clarified. Finally, I would like to pass on some new information that has just now come to our attention: due to complications that have arisen involving the disposal plant relocation, the scheduled move has been postponed for one month."

The assembly was thrown into a commotion, and most of the voices were protesting the announcement.

Each of the invited parties stood up and explained their positions. City Hall and the plant workers remained at loggerheads, and the school stated its hope for the prompt resolution of problems hindering the children's education. Still, the school sounded as if it were talking about total strangers, which frustrated Ms. Kotani and Mr. Adachi.

A mother said to be the representative of the local residents was the last person to stand up and speak.

"We just heard from the chairman that the relocation has been postponed one month. What on earth is the meaning of this?"

The complaint drew quite a bit of applause, and when someone heckled that they wanted a postponement of the postponement, the auditorium erupted in laughter.

"It's not as if we started our campaign for the relocation a couple of days ago! No! We've been collecting signatures and petitioning the city for four years!"

"That's right!"

"Exactly!"

The woman stared in the direction of the City Hall officials, and her voice grew shriller as she continued.

"You should try living in this school district. When you hang the wash out to dry, it gets covered with ash and black stains. Ash gets in your food during meals, and if you don't like it, you have to keep the windows closed, no matter how hot it gets. You've forced this horrible life on us—even though we pay our taxes—and then you pretend like you don't know anything about it. What do you mean there's gonna be a month's postponement because of complications? We've had enough of your making fools of us!"

The auditorium burst into applause again.

"Who caused the complications? Wasn't it you? Why do we have to suffer because of your complications? You talk about the city's side and the plant worker's side, but the people at the plant work for you, right? That means that they're your people. Why are you dragging us into a family feud that doesn't have anything to do with us? Don't you have any shame?"

This brought thunderous applause, and the City Hall representative made a sour face.

"Don't try to confuse the issue. We want only one thing, and that's for you to move the trash disposal plant as quickly as possible. There aren't any other problems. Inventing this dispute with the workers in order to drag in other issues is nothing more than a conspiracy."

"This concludes the statements from all the interested parties," said the chairman. "We will now begin debating the issues. If you would like to express your opinion, please raise your hand."

One of the mothers raised her hand.

"I completely agree with what Ms. Seko just said. There's never been a more blatant example of pollution than this. The lunch preparation room at the school has glass windows and screens. The screens are for when there are a lot of flies, and the glass is for when the ash is falling. The lunch mothers certainly have to go to a lot of trouble, but our school has to be much more careful about food preparation than other schools, and we, as parents, cannot very well ignore this problem. I don't think everyone in the school district should have to suffer just because there's a problem with how a small group is being treated. The larger group should be given priority."

Three other people stood up and said more or less the same thing.

"Is there anyone with a different opinion?" asked the chairman.

Someone towards the back raised his hand. It was Katsuichi's father.

"I've got a couple of questions I'd like to ask. The first I'd like to direct to the disposal plant people. Why do you have your cute little kids going on strike instead of going on strike yourselves? The second question is for Ms. Seko. What would you do if it were your kids that had to commute from the landfill?"

Tokuji's father stood up to reply to the first question.

"I'm not an educated man, and I can't say anything sophisticated or clever, so I'll just speak my mind. A while back, a Ms. Seko said that you shouldn't cause trouble for others over a family feud. Well, she's exactly right, and that's why we're not gonna strike. Workers got a right to strike, but we're hanging in there. By keeping our kids home from school, our own kids will fall behind in their studies, but we avoid causing trouble for everyone else. That's one reason we're doing it, but another reason is that as the saying goes, you can't sit idle when you're exposed to danger. If we end up living at the landfill, the kids are the ones that are gonna suffer, and we're teaching them that they gotta fight their own fights."

After this, Ms. Seko stood up.

"I'll answer the question put to me. If my children ended up having to commute from the landfill, I'd make a very clear distinction between my problem and other people's problems, and fight it on my own. I certainly wouldn't try to muddy the issue by pushing my personal feelings onto a grass-roots movement."

Katsuichi's father asked to speak again.

"Both opinions are natural enough, I suppose. But I'm more impressed with what the plant workers have to say. Too many mothers these days are overly concerned with what grades their kids are getting, and that speech would have done them some good. Trash comes from each and every one of us, and from each and every household, and we should all be responsible for disposing of our own waste. In the city, that's not really possible, and that's why we have disposal plants. But we should never forget whose trash it is, or we'll end being selfish about everything. In our zeal to get the disposal plant moved, we're forgetting that some other people might get hurt. I'm sure there's no one here who feels that as long as everything's okay for them, they could care less what happens to anybody else. And yet, we refuse to notice the misfortunes of the disposal plant people. The reason—as I said before—is that we've forgotten whose trash they're taking care of. So I want to make this crystal clear. If you think I'm gonna protect City Hall, you're sadly mistaken."

Katsuichi's father looked dead serious and had spoken in a loud voice.

"You tell 'em, Butcher," someone cheered.

Another person in the back raised a hand. Ms. Kotani craned her neck and saw that it was Junichi's mother.

"A little while ago, someone voiced the opinion that the majority shouldn't have to suffer for the convenience of the few. Two or three months ago, I probably would have said the same thing. My son is a first-grader, and he's rather sickly. He doesn't have many friends, and he used to spend all his time by himself. But about three months ago, something triggered a major change in him. What happened to my son can shed some light on the current situation, so I'd like to tell you about it.

"One day, my son's homeroom teacher took a mentally handicapped girl into their class. She was severely retarded: she couldn't speak clearly, and she had many toilet accidents. Not surprisingly, she took up a lot of the teacher's time, and classroom instruction suffered as a result. Many of us parents were worried that our kids were falling behind in their studies. In other words, we didn't think it was a good idea to sacrifice everyone for the sake of one child. Many other parents felt the same way, so we went to the school and protested. The teacher turned us down, and at the time, I couldn't help thinking how stubborn she was.

"But as time passed, I noticed a change taking place in my son. He started taking an interest in other people, and sometimes even seemed distressed over their problems. Before I knew it, those little first-graders had taken over the extremely difficult task of taking care of their new classmate. It might sound easy, but I have no doubt that those were extremely trying times for both the teacher and her students. We mothers were made to realize how, through that one ordeal, the children had grown as human beings.

"We thought that the majority shouldn't have to suffer for the few, but that was a mistake. When we shun the weak and the powerless, we become ruined as human beings. We should make the demands of the disposal plant people our demands, and we should make the children's struggle our struggle."

"That's right!" someone yelled. It was Mr. Adachi. Many in the audience applauded.

The meeting continued for about another hour, and many others stood up to voice their opinions. In the end, the opinions were reduced to two possible resolutions:

We, the local residents, in an appeal of dire emergency, demand the speedy and immediate implementation of the disposal plant relocation plan.

We, the local residents, strongly demand the relocation of the trash disposal plant. At the same time, we pledge our unequivocal support of the disposal plant workers in their struggle, and along with demanding the plant relocation, we vow to back them in their fight.

The two resolutions were put to a vote, and the second resolution was rejected by a margin of about three to one. Ms. Kotani was devastated. She learned a painful lesson on the complex nature of human beings and the cold truth of the world.

She made her way home with a heavy heart, and when she arrived, another depressing event was awaiting her: the second general meeting of the day. Her husband's parents, her own parents, and her husband were waiting for her.

All six of them sat down to dinner together, but an unpleasant and foreboding atmosphere hung in the air.

Her father was the first to speak.

"We're worried because we've heard that you two aren't getting on so well."

Ms. Kotani wanted to say that it wasn't a matter of getting along well, but of having two different outlooks on life.

"Maybe it's our fault," continued her father. "We let her take that job at the school because she's been so sheltered, and we thought she should get a taste of the real world for a couple of years. But maybe that was a mistake."

Her dad had it all wrong: society didn't exist just for her convenience.

"Fumi," said Ms. Kotani's mother-in-law, "we heard that you hate Kazuo staying out late trying to arrange things for the business."

"That's not true."

It wasn't true, and if her husband had been telling them that, then at least on this point, he was way out of line.

Recently, Ms. Kotani's husband had been coming home late, sometimes at two or three o'clock in the morning, drunk. But she wasn't the type to get annoyed by this sort of thing. She neither hated it, nor found it unpleasant.

"Today we had to impress some big shot," he had said one evening, "so we took him out to a cabaret and bought him a few rounds of drinks. I think we really pulled it off. Buttering up the business connections isn't easy work, you know. It's tough out there in the real world."

Ms. Kotani had felt like she was watching some sappy television drama.

"I don't think this is the time to mention how tough the real world is," she had told him. "You say it's tough buttering up connections, but from the look of you, I'd say you rather enjoyed yourself."

"That's pretty harsh," her husband had shot back at her. "Listen, you shouldn't be so blunt. I really hate women who talk like that."

Her mother-in-law continued.

"It's out of concern for your future that he's spending time going out with business associates."

"Of course. That's why, when his friends come by, I always receive them with a smile—no matter how tired I am."

"Fumi," said her mother-in-law, looking grave. "What is it about Kazuo that you don't like?"

Ms. Kotani remained silent. If she answered, her mother-in-law wouldn't understand, and it would only hurt her and her son's feelings. She could only think how difficult it was for two people with such different outlooks on life to live under the same roof. She had been racking her brains over that fact and just barely getting by. But she kept her thoughts locked in her heart.

The conversation droned on and on, but Ms. Kotani endured the agony to the end.

25. Betrayal

When the second proposal was rejected at the PTA general meeting, Mr. Adachi turned pale.

"This means we're gonna be on the defensive," he muttered to himself. A concrete materialization of his words was not long in coming.

Isao's father was called to City Hall and told that if he approved the move to the new residence, he would be hired as a permanent employee and appointed foreman. He promptly told them off, however, and the matter ended there.

The five teachers who distributed fliers were also called to City Hall. When they arrived, a supervisor from the Board of Education was waiting for them with one of the flyers in his hand.

"Are you the concerned teachers that are referred to in this flier?"

"Yes, we are."

"Just the five of you?"

"Yes, unfortunately there were only five of us."

The supervisor laughed, apparently amused at Mr. Adachi's way of answering.

"I admire your enthusiasm."

"Should we take that seriously?"

"Yes, of course."

"Well, then, thank you very much."

Ms. Kotani couldn't help but be amused by the repartee of these two sly dogs.

"Are you Ms. Fumi Kotani?"

"Yes, I am."

Her heart pounded at the thought of what he might say.

"You're Tetsuzo Usui's teacher, aren't you? I saw that story in the newspaper. That's quite a job you did there, and we appreciate your hard work. You're the main topic of conversation at the Board of Education these days."

She didn't know what to say to this, so she gave a slight bow.

"But then there's this flier. . . ."

She didn't think he was going to leave that out.

"I understand how you feel, but as public employees, who need to be neutral in these kind of situations, you've been a bit careless. Don't you agree?"

"Oh, I don't know," said Mr. Adachi, playing dumb.

"I only wanted the children to come back to school as quickly as possible. Is that so bad?" asked Ms. Kotani, with a straight face.

"I'm not saying it was bad. Quite the contrary, I'm deeply moved by your naiveté. But I think that naiveté is being taken advantage of politically."

"Oh, is that right?" replied Mr. Adachi. "Well, if that's what you're worried about, let me put your mind at ease. We might not look it, but we're incredible scoundrels. We sure as hell wouldn't be taken advantage of. If you like, we'd be happy to write out some sworn statements right now."

Mr. Adachi was really going after him, and this seemed to be throwing the supervisor off track.

"Mr. Adachi, you have the talent to become a principal or an assistant principal," said the supervisor, finally shooting back, "so you really should think about what you're saying."

The volley fell short of the mark, and Mr. Adachi brushed it off with a dismissive guffaw.

Ms. Kotani and the other teachers had been dreading a real chewing out, so they felt as if they had gotten off rather easy.

"There's all kinds of supervisors," Mr. Adachi warned them. "Some are hardheaded, and some are real pushovers. And they'll say just about anything. Be prepared for worse next time."

They left City Hall and dropped by the Teachers Union Office. Mr. Adachi talked to them for a long time.

"I know it's been tough since that resolution was rejected," he said, with a hearty laugh. "But you have to fight to keep the campaign going. Don't expect us to do all the work." Mr. Adachi played the hero no matter where he went.

After that, the five teachers headed over to the disposal plant, where they encountered a heartrending scene.

In front of Koji's house, a small truck was being loaded with various household effects, and the disposal plant people were gathered around, half-heartedly helping with the work. The children just stood there watching.

"What's goin' on? Is somebody moving?" Mr. Adachi casually

asked.

"Shhh!" said Tokuji's father, pulling him off to the side. The other teachers followed.

"That Senuma guy did this," said Tokuji's father with a pained expression. He threw up his arms in mock surrender. "He was told the same thing they told Isao's father. We tried to talk him out of it, but the bait was irresistible."

"Is that right?" said Mr. Adachi, with deep regret.

"Once we realized we couldn't talk him out of it, we decided we should see them off and not make a fuss. As Mr. Baku said, it's harder on the betrayer than on the betrayed. We had to agree, but that's why everyone's standing around like they're in limbo. It's painful for him if we help, yet we don't feel right if we don't. It's a strange feeling."

Mr. Orihashi and Mr. Ota were speechless.

They returned to the front of Koji's house to help, and as Mr. Adachi and Koji's father were carrying a dresser, their eyes met. Suddenly, Koji's father threw himself to the ground and prostrated himself at Mr. Adachi's feet.

"I'm sorry . . . I'm sorry . . . I'm sorry . . ."

The pathetic scene was too much for Ms. Kotani, and she averted her eyes.

Mr. Adachi bent down and took Koji's father's hand. Then he nodded several times in sympathy and quietly patted him on the back. Mr. Adachi's eyes were shining with tears.

They finished loading the truck.

"Let's go, Koji," said Koji's father.

Koji was lying in the corner of his empty room, with his face to the wall and a Styrofoam robot in his arms.

"Koji."

"I'm not going!" Koji screamed.

Koji's mother dragged him outside to the truck, and his eyes filled with tears.

"Koji," yelled Isao.

"Don't cry, Koji," said Jun, though he was crying himself.

Koji was forced into the truck, and all the other children started crying, too. But no one tried to prevent them from leaving, and the truck and Koji were soon speeding away, sending up a trail of white dust.

"Oh, Koji!" moaned Mr. Adachi like a wounded beast, and his sobbing seemed to flow from the bowels of the earth.

As tears of sympathy filled her eyes, Ms. Kotani realized that Mr. Adachi carried deep emotional scars, just like Mr. Baku.

The very next day, Mr. Adachi started a hunger strike. He set up a pup tent at the entrance to the disposal plant compound and plopped down on the ground sulkily.

On an old sheet, he had written "Now on Hunger Strike" and "Protesting the City's Callous Strike-Breaking Methods" in black and red paint. He had also written: "I'm a child of the sea. The disposal plant children aren't children of flies." Parodying a traditional children's song was typical of his brand of humor.

Mr. Adachi hadn't consulted with anyone, and when Mr.

Orihashi offered to join in the hunger strike, Mr. Adachi glared at him.

"I'm not trying to be a one-man hero," he said, turning him down. "I've got parents like everyone else. I want to be promoted, and I want to eat well. I'm scared of being reprimanded, and I'm even more scared of getting fired. I'm not even sure I won't be the next guy to betray you all. I'm just an ordinary human being, with his own history. History begets history, and confirms itself in the process."

With this puzzling statement, Mr. Adachi sent his friend away.

The first day of the hunger strike was difficult.

A steady stream of visitors tried to convince Mr. Adachi to abandon his strike, but he refused to listen and lay staring at the concrete wall in silence.

Between class periods, a student from Mr. Adachi's class reported to him. Mr. Adachi sat up as soon as he or she appeared, and then gave detailed instructions for the next period.

"Make sure you do a good job, okay?" he would say. "I don't want another teacher having to take care of you."

"Leave it to us, Mr. Adachi," the student would say cheerfully.

After the third period, another student came running up.

"The next period is lunch, Mr. Adachi," he said. "Want me to bring ya something?"

"Thank you, thank you," said Mr. Adachi, patting the boy on the head with a smile. "But if I ate, my strike would be meaningless."

In the afternoon, newspaper reporters started showing up, and Mr. Adachi spoke with them politely. He ended each discussion with the words, "Be sure to write the truth now."

Apart from the students and the newspaper reporters, he refused to speak to anyone. The only exception was when someone from the Teachers Union came to see him.

"Could you send a doctor from day three?" he asked. "I'm still too young to die."

At about three o'clock, there was a tapping sound coming from the other side of the wall. He turned to see what it was, and saw an eye peeping through a tiny hole.

"Who is it?"

"It's me. Isao."

"Isao?"

"Yeh. Are ya hungry?"

"Yeh, I'm hungry."

"It's pretty tough, isn't it?"

"Yes, it is. I usually eat like a pig, so it's pretty bad."

"Here, eat this."

Isao eased a rice ball through the hole, being careful not to let it get dirty.

"It's a rice ball, isn't it?"

"That's right."

"If I eat, it won't be a hunger strike."

"If you don't say anything, nobody'll know."

Mr. Adachi laughed.

"The doctor will know the second he looks at me," he said. "I'd like to eat it, but I better not."

"You can't have it, huh?"

Isao sounded disappointed, but the rice ball disappeared just as it had appeared.

"Isao."

"Huh?"

"For a hunger strike, it's okay to have water. If I don't drink any water at all, I'll be a dead man in two or three days. You got water at your house, don't you?"

"Yeh, we got as much as ya like."

"I don't mean tap water. I mean the water that comes in those two-liter bottles. Like the ones your dad drinks every night."

Isao seemed to understand.

"So fill up a cup with that and bring it here. And don't forget to bring a straw, too. A cup won't fit through this hole."

He heard the pitter-patter of many feet scurrying off. Apparently, Isao wasn't alone.

Before long, there was another tapping signal.

"How'd it go?"

"I got some."

"You filled it to the top?"

"Yeh, I filled it to the top."

"Great. Okay, so bring it up to the hole. That's a boy. Now pass me the straw."

Still lying down, Mr. Adachi took the straw in his mouth.

"Okay, put your end in."

"Yeh, it's in."

"Great."

Mr. Adachi was in bliss.

"You did a great job," he said, slurping away like a baby.

"How's it taste, Mr. Adachi?"

"It's incredibly good. It's so good I think I'm gonna faint. My head's reeling."

He wasn't lying. After going without food all day, the rude stuff was a jolt to his system.

"You better not spill any," he said selfishly. "And do a good job tilting the cup."

"Mr. Adachi, what're ya singin'?"

"Huh?"

Mr. Adachi was singing *Kiso-bushi*, an upbeat festival song, as if he didn't have a care in the world.

At about four o'clock, Ms. Kotani and the other three teachers came to the disposal plant.

"Mr. Adachi, are you all right?" asked a worried Ms. Kotani.

"Yes, quite all right. Your dear friend is most hale and hearty," said Mr. Adachi, sounding like the Humble Samurai. The cup of water had revived his spirits.

"Mr. Adachi, Junichi's mother and some others are going to go around asking for signatures. She says that when you talk to people individually, they're more understanding."

"That'd be a big help."

"She also said that she was going to contact the parents of your students and get them to help, too."

"That'd be an even bigger help," said Mr. Adachi, somewhat cheered by the news.

26. Shooting Stars

Mr. Adachi's hunger strike had widespread repercussions. Truancy was common enough in Japan, but a teacher going on a hunger strike out of sympathy for his truant students was unprecedented.

Some looked upon his actions favorably and pointed out that you don't see such passionate teachers nowadays. Others argued that dangerous teachers like him were the cause of society's problems. As for those at the Board of Education, they knew Mr. Adachi's motives and were at a loss as to how to deal with him.

Mr. Adachi himself simply remained silent and continued his hunger strike. He looked as if he were either lost in reflection or just enduring the pain. Passers-by viewed him as some kind of oddity of nature. Others merely pitied him.

A communication came in from Ms. Kotani. In a hastily scrawled note, she explained that their campaign was named "Parents in Support of the Disposal Plant Children" and that they had gotten even more signatures than expected. She added that Mr. Adachi's hunger strike had given many of the mothers quite a shock.

If they could get a majority of the parents to sign the petition, they would be able to overturn the previous vote. Mr. Adachi gave a little smile when he read the memo.

"I really want to eat some tempura," he murmured.

At about that time, there was a small incident at the school.

When Ms. Murano entered her classroom for the second period class, Koji was sitting in his old seat.

"Oh, dear!" she said in surprise. Koji had transferred to another school, so she couldn't understand why he was there.

"Koji, what's wrong?"

Koji silently put his school supplies in the desk.

"Oh? You want to study?"

"Yeh," said Koji, nodding.

"Did you walk all the way from the landfill?"

"Yeh."

Ms. Murano was shocked. For a little boy like Koji, such a trip would have taken at least an hour.

"Do your parents know you're here?"

He didn't answer, which meant it must have been his own idea.

"Koji, you've changed schools, so you have to go to your new school," said Ms. Murano, but out of consideration for his feelings that was the strongest thing she could say.

Koji attended classes through the fifth period.

When the class was over, Ms. Murano said, "Koji, starting tomorrow, I want you to be a good boy and go to your new school. I'm going to miss you, but this is something very important that both schools have agreed on. Okay?"

Koji stared down at the ground. Ms. Murano felt sorry for him and patted him on the head.

As soon as school let out, Koji smiled and dashed off to the disposal plant. When Mr. Adachi noticed someone approaching, he turned and found Koji standing there with a big grin on his face.

"Oh, it's Koji," said Mr. Adachi, instinctively reaching out to him.

Koji giggled and slammed into Mr. Adachi with all his weight. Weak with hunger, Mr. Adachi tumbled back helplessly, and Koji fell on top of him. Laughing, they wrestled together playfully.

"Hey, Koji, what's that?" asked Mr. Adachi, nodding towards his school bag.

"I went to school today."

"School? You mean Himematsu Elementary?"

"Yeh."

"I guess you're trying hard, too," said Mr. Adachi, musing over Koji's troubles.

Koji ran into the disposal plant compound. Like a baseball player who had hit a home run, he was warmly greeted with enthusiastic pats all over his body. Mr. Adachi came walking up behind him.

"I wonder what kind of world it'll be when you guys grow up?" he said, inspired by the scene.

Koji played happily at the disposal plant until evening, but when the sun started to set, he looked absolutely miserable. The other children knew what he was thinking.

"Koji, are ya headin' home now?" asked Isao, to cheer him up.

"Yeh," said Koji, cheerlessly.

"Hey, you guys, let's take him home. What'd ya say?"

"Yeh, let's take him home."

The children gathered around Koji and started running. They knew it would be pitch-dark for their trip back, but out of consideration for Koji's feelings, they didn't voice this worry.

They ran through the shopping district and crossed a busy highway. Singing together, they flew along like dragonflies. The sky was dyed deep red. When they reached the bridge that joined the old downtown area to the landfill, they stopped for a breather. Yoshikichi, who was overweight, was gasping for breath.

The ocean breeze felt cool against their overheated bodies, and the view of barges in the harbor looked like a brush stroke drawing.

"Let's get goin'," said Isao to the others.

"Yeh, let's do it," answered his comrades, dashing off with him.

When they entered the landfill, it stretched out before them like a desert.

"Wow!"

"It's huuuuuge!"

"It's like the ocean!"

"Turn it into a park!"

The children exchanged glances and laughed. And then they started running again.

When they reached Koji's house, his mother was waiting for him half in tears, and when she saw that her son was okay, she jumped up angrily.

"Ms. Senuma, don't get mad at him," yelled Isao, sticking his head through the window.

Several other heads popped up, too.

"Don't get mad at him, Ms. Senuma!" they yelled.

"So you brought Koji home, huh?"

"Yeh."

"And now you're going to walk all the way back to the disposal plant?"

"That's right."

It looked like Koji was off the hook.

"Mr. Senuma," called out Isao. "Koji came to Himematsu today."

"Is that so?"

Koji's parents exchanged glances.

"Koji, is that true?"

"It sure is," answered Koji candidly. "And I'm goin' there tomorrow, too."

"Mr. Senuma, don't make Koji leave us," said Keiko, staring straight at him.

"So Koji walked all the way to Himematsu Elementary?" muttered Koji's father, in a cheerless voice.

"Koji, we're gonna get goin'."

"Good-bye, Koji."

"Bye, Koji."

One after another, the children bade farewell. Koji's big,

brown eyes shined brightly, and he waved goodbye with all his might. Koji's father stood staring at the ground, as if lost in thought.

That same day, Ms. Kotani and the other teachers were extremely busy. Mr. Adachi was in the middle of a hunger strike, so they couldn't very well take their time in keeping the campaign going.

One of the mothers jokingly said that their supporters were multiplying like rabbits, and another mother showed them the following problem on geometric progression: if a male and female rabbit gave birth to twelve rabbits on New Year's Eve, and then a month later, each pair of rabbits gave birth to twelve more rabbits, and then the process continued for a year, how many rabbits would there be in December? The answer: 27,682,574,402 rabbits!

In other words, the campaign was conducted so that supporters would help gain more supporters. No wonder the numbers were multiplying so quickly.

"It's not enough that you understand the disposal plant children's plight," new supporters would say. "If we have your support, we need you to go out and persuade others." They concluded their talk by saying that they had much to learn from Ms. Kotani's students, who had befriended a mentally handicapped girl.

There were all kinds of households, and all kinds of parents. Two-income families, which had a hard time looking after their children, and parents who avoided school because their children had poor grades were quick to join the campaign. Parents that regularly attended observation classes and PTA meetings were not the only parents. Ms. Kotani and the other teachers talked about this when they returned to school.

The number of teachers helping to get signatures also gradually started to increase. Some only started hustling after being pressured by their students' parents.

Ms. Kotani bustled around until late at night and prayed that Mr. Adachi could hang in there a little bit longer. They had many mothers pulling for them.

It was late autumn, and the evenings were cold.

Mr. Adachi wrapped his blanket around him and gazed vacantly at the night sky. The stars were beautiful on cold nights—even in the city. The parents from the disposal plant had just come to talk to him. For some time now, they had stopped thanking him for his help. Such common politeness seemed overly formal towards such a close friend.

"Sure are a lot of shooting stars tonight," he absentmindedly whispered to himself.

Someone started knocking on the wall.

"Mr. Adachi, is anyone there?"

"Isao? No, nobody's here."

"Okay, then, I'll see ya on your side."

A few minutes later, Isao and the other children gathered around Mr. Adachi and made themselves at home. They sat or lay wherever they wanted.

"It's cold out here," said Mr. Adachi, as if criticizing them for coming.

"Well, we just ate dinner, so . . ." Tokuji began, but then he hurriedly shut his mouth.

"Don't worry about it," said Mr. Adachi, with a feeble laugh.

"We took Koji home," said Isao.

"Is that right? That was nice of you."

"Is it pretty tough, Mr. Adachi?" said Jun, somewhat timidly.

"Yeh, it's pretty painful," he answered, his eyelids drooping shut.

The children didn't know what to say, so they just stared at him.

"Oh, I just saw another shooting star. . ." said Mr. Adachi, meditatively. "I remember there were a lot of shooting stars that night, too."

"What night?"

"The first time I ever robbed anyone."

"Did you really rob somebody?" asked Misae, who was sitting at his feet.

"Yeh, I was dying from hunger like now, so I robbed somebody. Are you surprised?"

"Yeh," she answered, with a nod.

"Well, that's natural enough," he said, laughing and patting her on the head. "We only had about five teeny potatoes to eat a day."

"You must've been hungry."

"Yeh, I was starving and in pain like now. I had a big brother, and he was a really good brother like yours."

Jun looked down self-consciously.

"Well, I robbed places with my brother. We would sneak into warehouses and steal soybeans and corn and stuff. I was always terrified. Stealing is scary no matter how many times you do it."

"You did it that many times?" asked Shiro in a squeaky voice.

"It was too scary for me, so I stopped after four or five times, but my brother took it all in stride. He must have robbed tons of places. There were seven kids in our family, so he kept going out to get stuff for us—like a bird bringing food to the nest."

"Didn't the police ever catch him?"

"Yeh, he got caught quite a few times, but that didn't stop him. In the end, they hauled him off to a reformatory."

The children stared at Mr. Adachi in horror.

"That was the day he died."

Mr. Adachi said this rather casually, so the children didn't absorb the meaning at first.

"He used to love to read, just like your brother, Misae. When he died, they found a tattered copy of Seton's *Wild Animals I Have Known* in his pocket. He must've read it a thousand times."

Mr. Adachi looked off into the distance.

"Nobody can steal without feeling anything. I misunderstood my brother, and I've regretted it my entire life. I ate his life away. I'm alive today because I fed on my brother's life."

The children listened in dead silence.

"But not just me. We all live by feeding on the lives of others. We feed on those who die in war, and we feed on those killed for protesting war. Some people can feed on those lives without a passing thought, but for others, it causes a lot of suffering."

Mr. Adachi closed his eyes again.

"Your poor brother!" said Misae, whimpering softly.

Mr. Adachi gave her a gentle hug.

"You've got a pure heart," he said. "Hey, look at that! Another shooting star! That's my brother! He had a pure heart, too."

The children gazed up at the sky together.

The stars, clinging to the evening sky, glistened endearingly like fish eyes.

Epilogue

The sky looked especially expansive that morning, and the few remaining clouds looked like they had been sketched in with a brush. A pair of birds, perhaps black-eared kites, flirted with each other and flew off to the west.

The children were studying at their fort, but they took a short break to look up at the sky.

"Wow, it's so wide!"

They gazed up at the sky in wonder.

"Darn! Those kites really got it made!"

"Yeh, they're cuttin' school to go on a date," said Yoshikichi, jealously.

The kites shrunk as small as peas, and then faded into oblivion.

Just then, a small truck came puttering into the compound. It sounded different from the usual trash trucks, so the children turned to see what was going on. It was Koji! Perched on the top of the truck's load, he was waving to them with a big grin.

"It's Koji!"

"Koji's come back!"

The children jumped up together.

"Koji!"

It was no time for study. The children rushed off to see their friend, and Isao ran off to get Mr. Adachi.

"Mr. Adachi, it's Koji! Koji's returned!"

"Huh?"

Mr. Adachi was surprised, too. He tried to get up, but he tottered and nearly toppled over. Isao hurried over to support him.

"I'm okay, I'm okay," said Mr. Adachi, in a firm tone of voice.

Koji jumped down from the truck, and when he noticed Mr. Adachi, walking unsteadily with Isao's help, he darted off to see him.

"Mr. Adachi!" screamed Koji, jumping up on him.

"Whoa!"

Isao supported Mr. Adachi's body from behind, and Mr. Adachi caught Koji with an unexpected steadiness.

Koji giggled, and Mr. Adachi burst out laughing. The laughter welled up from the pit of his stomach, and he couldn't control himself.

At about noon, Ms. Kotani, Mr. Orihashi, and Mr. Ota came rushing to the disposal plant with flushed faces. The children and Mr. Adachi were all gathered around Koji at their fort.

"We did it! We did it!" yelled Mr. Ota, jumping up in the air.

"It looks like we've got more good news," said Mr. Adachi, to the children.

"You should be happy about this, Mr. Adachi. We got a majority of signatures."

"I don't believe it," said Mr. Adachi, his face breaking into a smile.

A majority of signatures meant that more than half of the households in the school district supported the disposal plant children. They didn't get the signatures from people on the street or from people who felt sorry for them. The people who had signed had actively joined the campaign. Ms. Kotani explained so that the children could understand.

"Through the mediation of the union and some city council members, negotiations have been scheduled for three o'clock this afternoon. Over two hundred mothers said they would be there for us."

Ms. Kotani turned towards the children.

"You're going to attend, too. They want to hear what you have to say."

"Just leave it to us," said Isao, beating his chest.

"Mr. Adachi, can you go, too?"

"I'm going even if it kills me," answered Mr. Adachi, cheerfully.

Ms. Kotani suddenly noticed Koji. His presence felt only natural, but something wasn't right about it.

"Oh, Koji!" she cried out. "You've come back!"

A big smile appeared on Koji's face.

"Now departin'!" yelled Isao.

The large cart started moving.

Mr. Adachi was limp from the three-day hunger strike, and he felt as if he didn't have a bone in his body. He could barely walk, so they had put him in the cart.

The cart sounded like it was singing. Rumble, rumble. Rumble, rumble. It wasn't a pretty song, but it sunk into your gut.

Tetsuzo held Ms. Kotani's hand tightly, and she occasionally glanced over at him. When she did, a bashful little smile broke out on his face. Then she returned his smile and gave his hand a little squeeze. When Tetsuzo squeezed back, they burst out laughing.

Mr. Baku smiled happily as he bobbed along after them. With Lucky pulling him along, he had to watch his steps. It gave him tremendous joy to watch Ms. Kotani and Tetsuzo playing their little game, and he whispered to Ryusei Kim that he was happy to have gone on living. He was looking forward to playing the cello with his friend again, but Ryusei Kim would have to wait a little longer.

Misae and Keiko each held one of Mr. Orihashi's hands. They chatted and laughed as they walked along together. Misae started to pout when Mr. Orihashi teased her, but she didn't stop walking. She just smacked him on the butt and kept going.

The cart continued singing its clumsy song. Rumble, rumble. Rumble, rumble. Isao, Jun, Tokuji, and Shiro pulled the cart, and Mr. Adachi dreamed about eating tempura. He still had to wait, but his eyes were shining. No doubt, he was imagining that he might be able to eat some today.

"What'd ya say?" asked Takeo, who was pushing the cart from behind.

"Oh, nothing, nothing," said Mr. Adachi, evasively.

He had been singing a children's song about rolling acorns, but Takeo thought he heard something about "rolling tempura."

Mr. Ota and Shigeko walked hand in hand like a couple and kept giggling over some secret or other. Yoshikichi made fun as he walked behind them.

The adults from the disposal plant walked along, too. They gazed upon their children fondly and upon the teachers with great trust.

The cart added a squeaking accompaniment to its rumbling song. Squeak, squeak. Rumble, rumble.

Koji walked alongside the cart, and Mr. Adachi occasionally patted him on the head. Koji's big brown eyes beamed with delight, and he smiled happily.

"We're off!" yelled Isao at the top of his lungs.

The cart picked up speed, and Lucky leapt up in response. Mr. Baku was yanked forward and nearly fell on his face.

He tried to yell for them to wait, but the words came out all garbled and incoherent. The children were startled and stopped the cart. Mr. Baku's face had shrunk to half its size and looked like a popped balloon. They were puzzled. Why had his face changed so suddenly?

Mr. Baku mumbled something and started searching the area frantically. Isao's father, who was standing nearby, realized what had happened.

"It's his dentures! Mr. Baku dropped his dentures!"

Everyone burst out laughing.

With everyone's help, the dentures were soon located. They were washed off with water, and Mr. Baku put them back in, returning to his former self.

Tetsuzo laughed aloud, and Ms. Kotani yanked his hand in disapproval—even though she herself couldn't fight back the laughter.

"Departing!" Isao yelled.

His stern voice was reminding them that it was too early for laughter. Everything still lay ahead.

Departing!

As Ms. Kotani held Tetsuzo's hand tightly, she reflected on the power of that word.

The cart once again began its clumsy song.

The End

Translator's Notes

1. Spoken primarily in Osaka, Kobe, and Kyoto, Kansai dialect is generally considered to be earthier and more direct than standard Japanese. Mr. Adachi and the disposal plant children usually speak in Kansai dialect.

2. Japan annexed Korea in 1910, shortly after the Russo-Japanese War (1904-5), and it remained a Japanese colony until the end of World War II, in 1945.

3. This is the actual name of the company, and the description attributed to Mr. Baku is historically accurate. Encouraged by the policies of Masatake Terauchi, the first governor-general of Korea, the company became the main corporation for swindling Koreans out of their land. The company eventually owned approximately 300,000 acres of land and "employed" 150,000 tenant farmers, who were the previous owners.

4. The hero of Soseki Natsume's novel of the same name, Botchan is a young and enthusiastic teacher, whose rebelliousness ends up getting him fired.